belisk

Bloodshed
and Three Novellas

Bloodshed
and Three Novellas

Cynthia Ozick

A Dutton Obelisk Paperback

E. P. DUTTON, INC. | NEW YORK

This paperback edition of Bloodshed and Three Novellas *first published in 1983 by E.P. Dutton.*

Reprinted by arrangement with Alfred A. Knopf, Inc.

Published in the United States by E.P. Dutton, Inc., 2 Park Avenue, New York, N.Y. 10016

Library of Congress Catalog Card Number: 83-70884

ISBN: 0-525-48065-X

Published simultaneously in Canada by Clarke, Irwin & Company Limited, Toronto and Vancouver

10 9 8 7 6 5 4 3 2 1

For Rachel, joy of my life

And for Gordon Lish,
who gave lodging to three of these four;
and who, while others gave reasons to conscience,
gave room to it

Contents

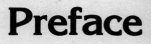

Preface

"**N**o Prefaces."

This maxim was given me by David Segal, my editor and heart's friend. We agreed on little, and had begun to diverge more and more, except on loving and liking. I am conscious now of what David would say, how once again I am refusing to listen to good advice. He thought of a Preface as a kind of apology, and his argument against introductory commentary for fiction was what lawyers call *res ipsa loquitur:* the thing speaks for itself. He saw fiction as an autonomous chariot in need of no ancillary vehicle: no fifth wheel for the real Apollo.

But if a book is a little, even only a very little, like a human life, what this Preface does is not countermand David, but copy him. He died young. If a human life is a little, even only a very little, like a book, he was all Preface. Which does not mean that he was only at the beginning, that he had "promise," that he was cut off at the start, that he had not yet really achieved; none of that; the opposite exactly. David himself teaches what a Preface can be. A Preface is not a tentative earliness, but a summation of ripeness. Or, to say it otherwise, a Preface explains what is to come; what was meant to materialize.

The materialization as it accrues is precious—who would wish for a life without hope of old age, who would wish for the *idea* of a story in place of the story itself? But the "what was meant" is worthwhile too—a short yet interesting life carries not simply intimations but constructs of the whole; and a story must not merely *be*, but mean.

Otherwise, what happens, in or out of literature, is only incident, not event. Incident is that inch of braid, the optic nerve. Event is the optic nerve's untangling report to the brain, djinn of wiliness and joy and judgment and lamentation. Had David lived, what we would have gone on to disagree about more and more was just this: incident versus event; experience versus consequence; deed versus outcome; feeling versus connecting; seeing versus seeing-into; or, to carry it as far as possible, art versus meaning. An even more grandiose way to describe this dispute is to call it Meaning in Fiction. I believe (though I don't intend anything so solemn or long-range as a Credo)—I believe that stories ought to judge and interpret the world. David in his own rich Preface both judged and interpreted the world. (He once explained Literature and Life to me: don't choose, he said; rather, choose both.)

There are four fictions in this short book. Three need no commentary; one does.

The three that do not are "Bloodshed," "An Education," and "A Mercenary." "An Education" is the first story I ever wrote, "A Mercenary" the last. A decade separates their composition. "Bloodshed" comes exactly in between.

"An Education" was written immediately after the completion of a long novel. That novel, the product of my education both as student and autodidact in the forties and fifties, cared about High Art and its issues; it was conceived in a style both "mandarin" and "lapidary," every paragraph a poem. In relief I turned to the stories of Frank O'Connor: how simple, how human, how comely and homely! Some of O'Connor's heroines are called Una; so is the protagonist of "An Education." O'Connor uses the whimsical triteness of ordinary speech; "An Education" yields "as the case might be," and "Una was impressed, not to say horrified."

Because of that "as the case might be," because of that "not to say," the author of the lapidary and mandarin novel stowed "An Education" in a box and did not take it out for years and years.

(O'Connor would not, I think, approve of an explanatory Preface either. In a Preface of his own, he once wrote: "I am probably more in the dark than my readers will be. One writes in a sort of dream, and I can only hope that when I awake, I shall be satisfied with what I have dreamt." This is perhaps as good a Credo as any. In the same Preface— though for the sake of accuracy I should point out that he calls it a Foreword—O'Connor tells that he was influenced by "the great Jewish storyteller, Isaac Babel." So it would not surprise him to learn that his Irish stories inspired a Jewish imitation.)

"A Mercenary" was stowed too, but only briefly. It has the kind of history a writer ought not to confess to: it brings peril. "A Mercenary" was undertaken in the middle of a summer with the notion that it would be a novel. What is the difference between a novel and a story or a novella? Not length (though some say length is the only difference), but maturation. The novel is long because it commences green and ignorant. The novel is long because it is a process, like chewing the apple of the Tree of Knowledge: it takes the novel a while before it discovers its human nakedness. The short forms are short because they begin with completion— with knowledge of nakedness. If the novella is the most captivating short form of all, it is because there is nothing more interesting than beginning with the end, nothing more mysterious than heading out to seek your fortune with your destination securely in your pocket. In the fairy tale, at the very outset of his journey, the Youngest Son receives from the magical crone an ordinary handkerchief—but spread it on the ground, and all manner of sweetmeats mob it. That is what the short forms do: you are in possession of your luck before you have gone half a mile.

Why is it perilous to say out loud that you aimed for a novel and were rewarded with a story? Someone is likely to argue, "Aha, see? You can *tell* that's a novel that got turned into a story," and that will be held against the writer, like the sin of transvestism. But you cannot make a novel out of a story, or a story out of a novel. What the novel requires is not length, but recognition. What the short forms require is not brevity, but realization. "A Mercenary" became a story the instant I understood that it *was* one.

"Bloodshed" comes out of a box after five years in hiding. What brought it out? Part of one sentence: ". . . the animals in all their majesty of health, shining hair, glinting hooves, timid nostrils, muscled like ourselves, gifted with tender eyes no different from our own, the whole fine creature trembling." And of that fragment of sentence, a single seductive phrase: "their majesty of health." For the sake of a handful of words, I pulled "Bloodshed" up out of the dark. It is no more than a particle of dream, like "Kubla Khan." Why had I buried it to begin with? On account of Chekhov, on account of Kafka.

There is a gun in "Bloodshed." Writing about writing, Chekhov instructs us that no gun should go off unless we have first been shown it hanging on the wall: every surprise must have its subliminal genesis. In "Bloodshed," two guns are shown, but they never go off; one is only a toy. This seems to me to be Chekhov's advice turned on its head. A gun is, after all, a teleology: it has an end, a purpose, a design. Robbed of its explosion, a story with a gun in it slides out of event (outcome), back into incident (unexplained conduct). To me, this is false Kafka-ism. It is all right if a genius like Kafka does not explain his Castle, but the rest of us are not geniuses and are obliged to explain our guns. Like the rebbe in "Bloodshed," I am more afraid of a gun that is "merely" a symbol than I am of one that can really go off. If I were inventing "Bloodshed" now, I would make Bleilip shoot someone; I think I even know whom. But it is too late: here is Bleilip, with his gun in his pocket, and it never goes off, at least not while we are with him.

Theron Raines, who read this story before anyone else, has persuaded me that the mysteriousness of Bleilip's intentions concerning his loaded gun is not the Chekhovian flaw I thought it to be, but is, rather, the rascally, crafty, cheating and evasive hand of the demonic. I am certain there *is* a demon in this tale; who he is I do not know; I hope he is not the Creator of the Universe, who admitted Auschwitz into His creation. And Auschwitz was so devised that, thanks to Zyklon B, not a drop of blood was made to flow; Auschwitz, with its toy showerheads, out of which no drop fell. ("It is the toy we have to fear," says the rebbe.)

I have arrived at "Usurpation," and if I am to continue to speak honestly, I had better acknowledge that the desire to explain "Usurpation" is the entire motive of all these paragraphs.

The necessary aspect of the explanation hardly includes citations, but since "Usurpation" is a usurper—its secondary title is "(Other People's Stories)"—it may be pertinent to mention its prey. The tale called "The Magic Crown" in my story is a paraphrase, except for a twist in its ending, of Malamud's "The Silver Crown"; the account of the disappointed messiah is Agnon's; and David Stern's "Agnon, A Story" is the mischievous seed of my metamorphosis of the Nobel Prize winner. I am indebted to David Stern also for an illuminating comment, in a conversation at Arthur Cohen's house, on the relation between the usurper and the idolator. (The "goat" I owe nothing to, having glimpsed him as a whitish blur at the Y one night, gripping his manuscript as he raced after his quarry.)

But the truth is that my aim here is less to pay homage than to respond to a bad review. "Usurpation" has had two prior publications—in a magazine, and in an annual anthology of stories. The latter was reviewed by an intelligent critic who was put off by "Usurpation" for a reason that puzzled me altogether. "I must admit," he wrote, "that I don't enjoy being tantalized. I want a story to *give* me something, not to tease me with possibilities. Technique as mystification, as a device for creating suspense, seems to me to be a sterile intellectual game."

I was astounded. I agreed with all his premises. Literature-as-game was exactly what I had been devotedly arguing against inside my mind for half a decade. Oh, I agreed! Hadn't I been suspicious of Bleilip's gun on that very ground —because it did not go off, because the explosion remained only a teasing possibility? But "Usurpation," though equally demonic, was in my view the opposite of mystery; it expressed not possibility but resolution. It was the incarnation of an *idea;* it had a purpose, it led to a point. I had seen the idea in all its alluring lucidity: why, then, had this fiction failed to engage the intelligent critic? I would not have minded had he said "Usurpation" was not his cup of tea; there are many kinds of stories, and no one can take pleasure in them all. But what he had said was that "Usurpation" was incomprehensible to him; he had accused me of mystification; and this was what troubled me, and still troubles me, and brings me to write these words.

"These words." They are English words. I have no other language. Since my slave-ancestors left off building the Pyramids to wander in the wilderness of Sinai, they have spoken a handful of generally obscure languages—Hebrew, Aramaic, twelfth-century French perhaps, Yiddish for a thousand years. Since the coming forth from Egypt five millennia ago, mine is the first generation to think and speak and write wholly in English. To say that I have been thoroughly assimilated into English would of course be the grossest understatement—what is the English language (and its poetry) if not my passion, my blood, my life? But that perhaps is overstatement. A language while we are zealously acquiring it can become a passion and a life. A language owned in the root of the tongue is loved without being the object of love: there is no sense of separateness from it. Do I love my eyeballs? No; but sight is everything.

Still, though English is my everything, now and then I feel cramped by it. I have come to it with notions it is too parochial to recognize. A language, like a people, has a history of ideas; but not *all* ideas; only those known to its experience. Not surprisingly, English is a Christian language. When I write English, I live in Christendom.

But if my postulates are not Christian postulates, what then?

In general, a piece of imaginative writing that cannot make its principles plain without a set of notes is justifiably regarded as a failure. Stories cannot carry suitcases stuffed with elucidations. They must speak for themselves, as David said, or go under. Why, then, is *The Waste Land*, the greatest modern poem, not permitted to speak for itself? Why does Eliot attach a suitcase full of footnotes? Because he has sent a net out to the sea of another civilization—what would Chaucer make of "*shantih*"?

There is no way to hear the oceanic amplitudes of the Jewish Idea in any single English word or phrase. "Judaism" is a Christian term, descriptive of something meanly sectarian and inferior: one "ism" out of many. English, which yields the historically distorted and singularly false "pharisaical," cannot be expected to naturalize the life-giving grandeur of the Hebrew word—yet how much more than word it is!—"Torah." And without "Torah," a Jew writing in English is reduced to the querulous apartness of an "ism." "Torah" is a stranger in English, and while English, famously eclectic and hospitable, will not oppress it (as once it oppressed the Pharisees), it cannot comfortably accommodate it.

So it came to me what the difficulty was: I had written "Usurpation" in the language of a civilization that cannot imagine its thesis.

One of the wraiths who briefly make an appearance in "Usurpation" is the ghost of Ibn Gabirol, an eleventh-century Spanish Jewish philosopher and poet; he wrote in Hebrew and Arabic. What I did not know while I was inventing "Usurpation"—I found it out nearly two years later, from a Spanish medievalist in Ohio—is that Ibn Gabirol himself had worried over the theme that obsesses my tale. To offer it as succinctly as possible, the worry is this: whether Jews ought to be storytellers. Conceive of Chaucer fretting over whether Englishmen should be storytellers!

There is One God, and the Muses are not Jewish but Greek. Ibn Gabirol wondered whether the imagination itself —afflatus, trance, and image—might offend the Second Commandment. "Usurpation" wonders the same. Does the Commandment against idols warn even ink?

Belief in idols is belief in magic. And storytelling, as

every writer knows, is a kind of magic act. Or Eucharist, wherein the common bread of language assumes the form of a god.

"Usurpation" is a story written against story-writing; against the Muse-goddesses; against Apollo. It is against magic and mystification, against sham and "miracle," and, going deeper into the dark, against idolatry. It is an invention directed against inventing—the point being that the story-making faculty itself can be a corridor to the corruptions and abominations of idol-worship, of the adoration of magical event.

How can Christianity—itself a story of magic, a miracle story—take that in? How can English, this Christian tongue, release it?

It came to me that if only I had been able to write "Usurpation" in a Jewish language—Hebrew or Yiddish, or, say, the Ladino spoken by Ibn Gabirol's descendants—it would have been understood instantly. No one would suppose it to be a story that leads nowhere, with no point.

At the close of "Usurpation," the ghost of the poet Tchernikhovsky, translated to Paradise, clearly chooses the company of Canaanite idols; in life, Tchernikhovsky chose the god of poetry, Apollo. The Canaanite idols are predictably (what else could they be?—given the career of Abraham, who rejected them forever) anti-Semitic.

Canaanite babies were regularly sacrificed to fanciful clay forms. But the old cannibal-gods still inhabit the earth. The genius of Abraham and Moses has never taken hold. The deep pity of the Second Commandment is treated as null and void. Human sacrifice to this and that fantasy continues to teem on the planet. The chief religion of the West has as its centerpiece an incident of human sacrifice, presented as a philosophical and metaphysical good. And only the other day a profoundly humane writer I know praised the god of Revolution for "merely" driving the people of the Cambodian cities out onto the roads: how much more humane this was than any previous exaction of this god of the ideal! She was comforted, and given evidence of the progress of societies.

"Usurpation" is about the dread of Moloch, the dread of lyrical faith, the dread of metaphysics, the dread of "theology," the dread of fantasy and fancy, of god and Muse; above all the dread of idols; the dread of the magic that kills. The dread of imagination.

Ibn Gabirol felt the same; and wrote poems.

Why do we become what we most desire to contend with?

Why do I, who dread the cannibal touch of story-making, lust after stories more and more and more?

Why do demons choose to sink their hooves into black, black ink?

As if ink were blood.

May 30, 1975

A Mercenary

*Today we are all expressionists—men who
want to make the world outside themselves
take the form of their life within themselves.*

—JOSEPH GOEBBELS

Stanislav Lushinski, a Pole and a diplomat, was not a Polish diplomat. People joked that he was a mercenary, and would sell his tongue to any nation that bargained for it. In certain offices of the glass rectangle in New York he was known as "the P.M."—which meant not so much that they considered him easily as influential as the Prime Minister of his country (itself a joke: his country was a speck, no more frightening than a small wart on the western—or perhaps it was the eastern—flank of Africa), but stood, rather, for Paid Mouthpiece.

His country. Altogether he had lived in it, not counting certain lengthy official and confidential visits, for something over fourteen consecutive months, at the age of nineteen—that was twenty-seven years ago—en route to America. But though it was true that he was not a native, it was a lie that he was not a patriot. Something in that place had entered him, he could not shake out of his nostrils the musky dreamy fragrance of nights in the capital—the capital was, as it happened, the third-largest city, though it had the most sophisticated populace. There, his colleagues claimed, the men wore trousers and the women covered their teats.

The thick night-blossoms excited him. Born to a flag-stoned Warsaw garden, Lushinski did not know the names of flowers beyond the most staid dooryard sprigs, daisies and roses, and was hardly conscious that these heaps of petals, meat-white, a red as dark and boiling as an animal's maw, fevered oranges and mauves, the lobe-leafed mallows, all

hanging downward like dyed hairy hanged heads from tall
bushes at dusk, were less than animal. It was as if he dis-
believed in botany, although he believed gravely enough in
jungle. He felt himself native to these mammalian perfumes,
to the dense sweetness of so many roundnesses, those round
burnt hills at the edge of the capital, the little round brown
mounds of the girls he pressed down under the trees—he,
fresh out of the roil of Europe; they, secret to the ground,
grown out of the brown ground, on which he threw himself,
with his tongue on their black-brown nipples, learning their
language.

He spoke it not like a native—though he was master of
that tangled clot of extraordinary inflections scraped on the
palate, nasal whistles, beetle-clicks—but like a preacher.
The language had no written literature. A century ago a
band of missionaries had lent it the Roman alphabet and
transcribed in it queer versions of the Psalms, so that

> thou satest in the throne judging right

came out in argot:

> god squat-on-earth-mound
> tells who owns
> accidentally-decapitated-by-fallen-tree-trunk
> deer,

and it was out of this Bible, curiously like a moralizing hunt-
ing manual, the young Lushinski received his lessons in syn-
tax. Except for when he lay under a cave of foliage with a
brown girl, he studied alone, and afterward (he was still
only approaching twenty) translated much of Jonah, which
the exhausted missionaries had left unfinished. But the story

of the big fish seemed simple-minded in that rich deep tongue, which had fifty-four words describing the various parts and positions of a single rear fin. And for "prow" many more: "nose-of-boat-facing-brightest-star," or star of middle dimness, or dimmest of all; "nose-of-boat-fully-invisible-in-rain-fog"; half-visible; quarter-visible; and so on. It was an observant, measuring, meticulous language.

His English was less given to sermonizing. It was diplomat's English: which does not mean that it was deceitful, but that it was innocent before passion, and minutely truthful about the order of paragraphs in all previous documentation.

He lived, in New York, with a mistress: a great rosy woman, buxom, tall and talkative. To him she was submissive.

In Geneva—no one could prove this—he lived on occasion with a strenuous young Italian, a coppersmith, a boy of twenty-four, red-haired and lean and not at all submissive.

His colleagues discovered with surprise that Lushinski was no bore. It astounded them. They resented him for it, because the comedy had been theirs, and he the object of it. A white man, he spoke for a black country: this made a place for him on television. At first he came as a sober financial attaché, droning economic complaints (the recently expelled colonial power had exploited the soil by excessive plantings; not an acre was left fallow; the chief crop—jute? cocoa? rye? Lushinski was too publicly fastidious ever to call it by its name—was thereby severely diminished, there was famine in the south). And then it was noticed that he was, if one listened with care, inclined to obliqueness—to, in fact, irony.

It became plain that he could make people laugh. Not that he told jokes, not even that he was a wit—but he began to recount incidents out of his own life. Sometimes he was believed; often not.

In his office he was ambitious but gregarious. His assistant, Morris Ngambe, held an Oxford degree in political science. He was a fat-cheeked, flirtatious young man with a glossy bronze forehead, perfectly rounded, like a goblet. He was exactly half Lushinski's age, and sometimes, awash in papers after midnight, their ties thrown off and their collars undone, they would send out for sandwiches and root beer (Lushinski lusted after everything American and sugared); in this atmosphere almost of equals they would compare boyhoods.

Ngambe's grandfather was the brother of a chief; his father had gone into trade, aided by the colonial governor himself. The history and politics of all this was murky; nevertheless Ngambe's father became rich. He owned a kind of assembly-line consisting of many huts. Painted gourds stood in the doorways like monitory dwarfs; these were to assure prosperity. His house grew larger and larger; he built a wing for each wife. Morris was the eldest son of the favorite wife, a woman of intellect and religious attachment. She stuck, Morris said, to the old faith. A friend of Morris's childhood —a boy raised in the missionary school, who had grown up into a model bookkeeper and dedicated Christian—accused her of scandal: instead of the Trinity, he shouted to her husband (his employer), she worshipped plural gods; instead of caring for the Holy Spirit, she adhered to animism. Society was progressing, and she represented nothing but regression: a backslider into primitivism. The village could not tolerate it, even in a female. Since it was fundamental propriety to ignore wives, it was clear that the fellow was crazy to raise a fuss over what one of a man's females thought or did. But it was also fundamental propriety to ignore an insane man (in argot the word for "insane" was, in fact, "becoming-childbearer," or, alternatively, "bottom-hole-mouth"), so everyone politely turned away, except Morris's mother, who followed a precept of her religion: a female who has a man (in elevated argot "lord") for her enemy must offer him her loins in reconciliation. Morris's mother came naked at night to her accuser's hut and parted her legs for him on the floor. Earlier he had been sharpening pencils; he took the knife from his pencil-pot (a gourd hollowed-out and painted, one of Morris's father's most successful export items) and stabbed her breasts. Since she had recently given birth (Morris was twenty years older than his youngest brother), she bled both blood and milk, and died howling, smeared pink. But because in her religion the goddess Tanake declares before five hundred lords that she herself became divine through having been cooked in her own milk, Morris's mother, with her last cry, pleaded for similar immortality; and so his father, who was less pious but who had loved her profoundly, made a feast. While the governor looked the other way, the murderer was murdered; Morris was unwilling to describe the execution. It was, he said in his resplendent Oxonian voice, "very clean." His mother was ceremonially eaten; this accomplished her transfiguration. Her husband and eldest son were obliged to share the principal sacrament, the nose, "emanator-of-wind-of-birth." The six other wives—Morris called each of them Auntie—divided among them a leg steamed in goat's milk. And everyone who ate at that festival, despite the plague of gnats that attended the day, became lucky ever after. Morris was admitted to Oxford; his grandfather's brother died at a very great age and his father replaced him as chief; the factory acquired brick buildings and chimneys and began manufacturing vases both of ceramic and glass; the colonial power was thrown out; Morris's mother was turned into a goddess, and her picture sold in the villages. Her name had been Tuka. Now she was Tanake-Tuka, and could perform miracles for devout women, and sometimes for men.

Some of Ngambe's tales Lushinski passed off as his own observations of what he always referred to on television as "bush life." In the privacy of his office he chided Morris for having read too many Tarzan books. "I have only seen the movies," Ngambe protested. He recalled how in London on Sunday afternoons there was almost nothing else to do. But he believed his mother had been transformed into a divinity. He said he often prayed to her. The taste of her flesh had bestowed on him simplicity and geniality.

From those tedious interviews by political analysts Lushinski moved at length to false living rooms with false "hosts" contriving false conversation. He felt himself recognized, a foreign celebrity. He took up the habit of looking caressingly into the very camera with the red light alive on it, signaling it was sensitive to his nostrils, his eyebrows, his teeth and his ears. And under all that lucid theatrical blaze, joyful captive on an easy chair between an imbecile film reviewer and a cretinous actress, he began to weave out a life.

Sometimes he wished he could write out of imagination: he fancied a small memoir, as crowded with desires as with black leafy woods, or else sharp and deathly as a blizzard; and at the same time very brief and chaste, though full of horror. But he was too intelligent to be a writer. His intelligence was a version of cynicism. He rolled irony like an extra liquid in his mouth. He could taste it exactly the way Morris tasted his mother's nose. It gave him powers.

He pretended to educate. The "host" asked him why he, a white man, represented a black nation. He replied that

Disraeli too had been of another race, though he led Britain. The "host" asked him whether his fondness for his adopted country induced him to patronize its inhabitants. This he did not answer; instead he hawked up into the actress's handkerchief—leaning right over to pluck it from her décolletage where she had tucked it—and gave the "host" a shocked stare. The audience laughed—he seemed one of those gruff angry comedians they relished.

Then he said: "You can only patronize if you are a customer. In my country we have no brothels."

Louisa—his mistress—did not appear on the programs with him. She worried about his stomach. "Stasek has such a very small stomach," she said. She herself had oversized eyes, rubbed blue over the lids, a large fine nose, a mouth both large and nervous. She mothered him and made him eat. If he ate corn she would slice the kernels off the cob and warn him about his stomach. "It is very hard for Stasek to eat, with his little stomach. It shrank when he was a boy. You know he was thrown into the forest when he was only six."

Then she would say: "Stasek is generous to Jews but he doesn't like the pious ones."

They spoke of her as a German countess—her last name was preceded by a "von"—but she seemed altogether American, though her accent had a fake melody either Irish or Swedish. She claimed she had once run a famous chemical corporation in California, and truly she seemed as worldly as that, an executive, with her sudden jagged gestures, her large hands all alertness, her curious attentiveness to her own voice, her lips painted orange as fire. But with Lushinski she could be very quiet. If they sat at some party on opposite sides of the room, and if he lifted one eyebrow, or less, if he twitched a corner of his mouth or a piece of eyelid, she understood and came to him at once. People gaped; but she was proud. "I gave up everything for Stanislav. Once I had three hundred and sixty people under me. I had two women who were my private secretaries, one for general work, one exclusively for dictation and correspondence. I wasn't always the way you see me now. When Stasek tells me to come, I come. When he tells me to stay, I stay."

She confessed all this aloofly, and with the panache of royalty. On official business he went everywhere without her. It was true his stomach was very flat. He was like one of those playing-card soldiers in *Alice in Wonderland*: his shoulders a pair of neat thin corners, everything else cut along straight lines. The part in his hair (so sleekly black it looked painted on) was a clean line exactly above the terrifying pupil of his left eye. This pupil measured and divided, the lid was as cold and precise as the blade of a knife. Even his nose was a rod of machined steel there under the live skin—separated from his face, it could have sliced anything. Still, he was handsome, or almost so, and when he spoke it was necessary to attend. It was as if everything he said was like that magic pipe in the folktale, the sound of which casts a spell on its hearers' feet and makes the whole town dance madly, willy-nilly. His colleagues only remembered to be scornful when they were not face to face with him; otherwise, like everybody else, they were held by his mobile powerful eyes, as if controlled by silent secret wheels behind, and his small smile that was not a smile, rather a contemptuous little mock-curtsy of those narrow cheeks, and for the moment they believed anything he told them, they believed that his country was larger than it seemed and was deserving of rapt respect.

In New York Morris Ngambe had certain urban difficulties typical of the times. He was snubbed and sent to the service entrance (despite the grandeur of his tie) by a Puerto Rican elevator man in an apartment house on Riverside Drive, he was knocked down and robbed not in Central Park but a block away by a gang of seven young men wearing windbreakers reading "Africa First, Harlem Nowhere"— a yellow-gold cap covering his right front incisor fell off, and was aesthetically replaced by a Dr. Korngelb of East Forty-ninth Street, who substituted a fine white up-to-date acrylic jacket. Also he was set upon by a big horrible dog, a rusty-furred female chow, who, rising from a squat, having defecated in the middle of the sidewalk, inexplicably flew up and bit deep into Morris's arm. Poor Morris had to go to Bellevue outclinic for rabies injections in his stomach. For days afterward he groaned with the pain. "This city, this city!" he wailed to Lushinski. "London is boring but at least civilized. New York is just what they say of it—a wilderness, a jungle." He prayed to his mother's picture, and forgot that his own village at home was enveloped by a rubbery skein of gray forest with all its sucking, whistling, croaking, gnawing, perilously breathing beasts and their fearful eyes luminous with moonlight.

But at other times he did not forget, and he and Lushinski would compare the forests of their boyhoods. That sort of conversation always made Morris happy: he had been gifted with an ecstatic childhood, racing with other boys over fallen berries, feeling the squush of warm juice under his swift toes, stopping to try the bitter taste of one or two; and once they swallowed sour flies, for fun, and on a dare. But mostly there were games—so clever and elaborate he wondered at them even now, who had invented them, and in what inspired age long ago: concealing games, with complicated clue-songs attached, and quiet games with twigs of different sizes from different kinds of bark, requiring as much concentration as chess; and acrobatic games, boys suspended upside down from branches to stretch the muscles of the neck, around which, one day, the great width of the initiation-band would be fitted; and sneaking-up games, mimicking the silence of certain deer-faced little rodents with tender flanks who streaked by so quickly they could be perceived only as a silver blur. And best of all, strolling home after a whole dusty day in the bright swarm of the glade, insects jigging in the slotted sunbeams and underfoot the fleshlike fever-pad of the forest floor; and then, nearing the huts, the hazy smell of dusk beginning and all the aunties' indulgent giggles; then their hearts swelled: the aunties called them "lord"; they were nearly men. Morris—in those days he was Mdulgo-kt'dulgo ("prime-soul-born-of-prime-soul")—licked the last bit of luscious goat-fat from his banana leaf and knew he would one day weigh in the world.

Lushinski told little of his own forest. But for a moment its savagery wandered up and down the brutal bone of his nose.

"Wolves?" Morris asked; in his forest ran sleek red jackals with black swaths down their backs, difficult to trap but not dangerous if handled intelligently, their heads as red as some of these female redheads one saw taking big immodest strides in the streets of London and New York. But wolves are northern terrors, Slavic emanations, spun out of snow and legends of the Baba Yaga.

"Human wolves," Lushinski answered, and said nothing after that. Sometimes he grew sullen all at once, or else a spurt of fury would boil up in him; and then Morris would think of the chow. It had never been determined whether the chow was rabid or not. Morris had endured all that wretchedness for nothing, probably. Lulu (this was Louisa: a name that privately disturbed Morris—he was ashamed to contemplate what these two horrid syllables denoted in argot, and prayed to his mother to help him blot out the pictures that came into his thoughts whenever Lushinski called her on the telephone and began with—O Tanake-Tuka!—"Lulu?")—Lulu also was sometimes bewildered by these storms which broke out in him: then he would reach out a long hard hand and chop at her with it, and she would remember that once he had killed a man. He had killed; she saw in him the power to kill.

On television he confessed to murder:

Once upon a time, long ago in a snowy region of the world called Poland, there lived a man and his wife in the city of Warsaw. The man ruled over a certain palace—it was a bank—and the woman ruled over another palace, very comfortable and rambling, with hundreds of delightful story-books behind glass doors in mahogany cases and secret niches to hide toy soldiers in and caves under chairs and closets that mysteriously connected with one another through dark and enticing passageways—it was a rich fine mansion on one of the best streets in Warsaw. This noble and blessed couple had a little son, whom they loved more than their very lives, and whom they named Stanislav. He was unusually bright, and learned everything more rapidly than he could be taught, and was soon so accomplished that they rejoiced in his genius and could not get over their good luck in having given life to so splendid a little man. The cook used to bring him jigsaw puzzles consisting of one thousand pieces all seemingly of the same shape and color, just for the marvel of watching him make a picture out of them in no time at all. His father's chauffeur once came half an hour early, just to challenge the boy at chess; he was then not yet five, and the maneuvers he invented for his toy soldiers were amusingly in imitation of the witty pursuits of the chessboard. He was already joyously reading about insects, stars, and trolley cars. His father had brought home for him one evening a little violin, and his mother had engaged a teacher of celebrated reputation. Almost immediately he began to play with finesse and ease.

In Stanislav there was only one defect—at least they thought it a defect—that grieved his parents. The father and mother were both fair, like a Polish prince and a Polish princess; the mother kept her golden hair plaited in a snail-like bun over each pink ear, the father wore a sober gray waistcoat under his satiny pink chin. The father was ruddy, the mother rosy, and when they looked into one another's eyes, the father's as gray as the buttery gray cloth of his vest, the mother's as clamorously blue as the blue chips of glass in her son's kaleidoscope, they felt themselves graced by God with such an extraordinary child, indeed a prodigy (he was obsessed by an interest in algebra)—but, pink and ruddy and golden and rosy as they were, the boy, it seemed, was a gypsy. His hair was black with a slippery will of its own, like a gypsy's, his eyes were brilliant but disappointingly black, like gypsy eyes, and even the skin of his clever small hands had a dusky glow, like gypsy skin. His mother grew angry when the servants called him by a degrading nickname— Ziggi, short for *Zigeuner*, the German word for gypsy. But when she forbade it, she did not let slip to them that it was the darkness she reviled, she pretended it was only the German word itself; she would not allow German to be uttered in that house—German, the language of the barbarian invaders, enemies of all good Polish people.

All the same, she heard them whisper under the stairs, or in the kitchen: *Zigeuner*; and the next day the Germans came, in helmets, in boots, tanks grinding up even the most fashionable streets, and the life of the Warsaw palaces, the fair father in his bank, the fair mother under her rose-trellis, came to an end. The fair father and the fair mother sewed *zloty* in their underclothes and took the dark child far off into a peasant village at the edge of the forest and left him, together with the money to pay for it, in the care of a rough but kind-hearted farmer until the world should right itself again. And the fair blessed couple fled east, hoping to escape to Russia: but on the way, despite fair hair and pale eyes and aristocratic manners and the cultivated Polish speech of city people with a literary bent, they were perceived to be non-Aryan and were roped to a silver birch at the other end of the woods and shot.

All this happened on the very day Stanislav had his sixth birthday. And what devisings, months and months ahead of time, there had been for that birthday! Pony rides, and a clown in a silken suit, and his father promising to start him on Euclid. . . . And here instead was this horrid dirty squat-necked man with a bald head and a fat nose and such terrible fingers with thick horny blackened nails like angle irons, and a dreadful witchlike woman standing there with her face on fire, and four children in filthy smocks peering out of a crack in a door tied shut with a rubber strap.

"He's too black," said the witch. "I didn't know he'd be a black one. You couldn't tell from the looks of *them*. He'll expose us, there's danger in it for us."

"They paid," the man said.

"Too black. Get rid of him."

"All right," said the man, and that night he put the boy out in the forest. . . .

But now the "host" interrupted, and the glass mouth of the television filled up with a song about grimy shirt collars and a soap that could clean them properly. "Ring around the collar," the television sang, and then the "host" asked, "Was that the man you killed?"

"No," Lushinski said. "It was somebody else."

"And you were only six?"

"No," Lushinski said, "by then I was older."

"And you lived on your own in the forest—a little child, imagine!—all that time?"

"In the forest. On my own."

"But how? How? You were only a child!"

"Cunning," Lushinski said. It was all mockery and parody. And somehow—because he mocked and parodied, sitting under the cameras absurdly smiling and replete with contradictions, the man telling about the boy, Pole putting himself out as African, candor offering cunning—an uneasy blossom of laughter opened in his listeners, the laughter convinced: he was making himself up. He had made himself over, and now he was making himself up, like one of those comedians who tell uproarious anecdotes about their preposterous relatives. "You see," Lushinski said, "by then the peasants wanted to catch me. They thought if they caught me and gave me to the Germans there would be advantage in it for them—the Germans might go easy on the village, not come in and cart away all the grain without paying and steal the milk—oh, I was proper prey. And then I heard the slaver of a dog: a big sick bulldog, I knew him, his name was Andor and he had chewed-up genitals and vomit on his lower jaw. He belonged to the sexton's helper who lived in a shed behind the parish house, a brute he was, old but a brute, so I took a stick when Andor came near and stuck it right in his eye, as deep as I could push it. And Andor comes rolling and yowling like a demon, and the sexton's helper lunges after him, and I grab Andor—heavy as a log, heavy as a boulder, believe me—I grab him and lift him and smash him right down against the sexton's helper, and he's knocked over on his back, by now Andor is crazy, Andor is screeching and sticky with a river of blood spilling out of his eye, and he digs his smelly teeth like spades, like spikes, like daggers, into the old brute's neck—"

All this was comedy: Marx Brothers, Keystone cops, the audience is elated by its own disbelief. The bulldog is a dragon, the sexton's helper an ogre, Lushinski is only a storyteller, and the "host" asks, "Then that's the man you killed?"

"Oh no, Jan's Andor killed Jan."

"Is it true?" Morris wanted to know—he sat in the front row and laughed with the rest—and began at once to tell about the horrid chow on East Ninetieth Street; but Lulu never asked this. She saw how true. Often enough she shook him out of nightmares, tears falling from his nostrils, his tongue curling after air with hideous sucking noises. Then she brought him hot milk, and combed down his nape with a wet hand, and reminded him he was out of it all, Poland a figment, Europe a fancy, he now a great man, a figure the world took notice of.

He told no one who the man was—the man he killed: not even Lulu. And so she did not know whether he had killed in the Polish forest, or in the camp afterward when they caught him, or in Moscow where they took him, or perhaps long afterward, in Africa. And she did not know whether the man he killed was a gypsy, or a Pole, or a German, or a Russian, or a Jew, or one of those short brown warriors from his own country, from whom the political caste was drawn. And she did not know whether he had killed with his hands, or with a weapon, or through some device or ruse. Sometimes she was frightened to think she was the mistress of a murderer; and sometimes it gladdened her, and made her life seem different from all other lives, adventurous and poignant; she could pity and admire herself all at once.

He took Morris with him to Washington to visit the Secretary of State. The Secretary was worried about the threat-

ened renewal of the northern tribal wars: certain corporate
interests, he explained in that vapid dialect he used on purpose to hide the name of the one furious man whose fear he
was making known, who had yielded his anxiety to the Secretary over a lunch of avocado salad, fish in some paradisal
sauce, wine-and-mushroom-scented roast, a dessert of sweetened asparagus mixed with peppered apricot liqueur and
surrounded by a peony-pattern of almond cakes—certain
corporate interests, said the Secretary (he meant his friend),
were concerned about the steadiness of shipments of the
single raw material vital to the manufacture of their indispensable product; the last outbreak of tribal hostility had
brought the cutting in the plantations to a dead halt; the
shippers had nothing to send, and instead hauled some
rotted stuff out of last year's discarded cuttings in the store-
houses; it wouldn't do, an entire American industry depended on peace in that important region; but when he said
"an entire American industry," he still meant the one furious
man, his friend, whose young third wife had been at the
luncheon too, a poor girl who carried herself now like a poor
girl's idea of a queen, with hair expensively turned stiff as
straw, but worth looking at all the same. And so again he
said "that important region."

"You know last time with the famine up there," the Secretary continued, "I remember twenty years or so ago, before your time, I was out in the Cameroon, and they were at
each other's throats over God knows what."

Morris said, "It was the linguistic issue. Don't think of
'tribes,' sir; think of nations, and you will comprehend better
the question of linguistic pride."

"It's not a matter of comprehension, it's a matter of
money. They wouldn't go to the plantations to cut, you see."

"They were at war. There was the famine."

"Mr. Ngambe, you weren't born then. If they had cut something, there wouldn't have been famine."

"Oh, that crop's not edible, sir," Morris protested: "it's like eating rope!"

The Secretary did not know what to do with such obtuseness; he was not at all worried about a hunger so far away which, full of lunch, he could not credit. His own stomach seemed a bit acid to him, he hid a modest belch. "God knows," he said, "what those fellows eat—"

But "Sir," said Lushinski, "you have received our documents on the famine in the south. The pressure on our northern stocks—believe me, sir, they are dwindling—can be alleviated by a simple release of Number Three grain deposits, for which you recall we made an appeal last week—"

"I haven't gotten to the Number Threes, Mr. Lushinski. I'll look them over this weekend, I give you my word. I'll put my staff right on it. But the fact is, if there's an outbreak—"

"Of cholera?" said Morris. "We've had word of some slight cholera in the south already."

"I'm talking about war. It's a pity about the cholera, but that's strictly internal. We can't do anything about it, unless the Red Cross . . . Now look here, we can't have that sort of interference again with cutting and with shipments. We can't have it. There has got to be a way—"

"Negotiations have begun between the Dt' and the Rundabi," Morris said; he always understood when Lushinski wished him to speak, but he felt confused, because he could feel also that the Secretary did not wish him to speak and was in fact annoyed with him, and looked to Lushinski only. All at once bitterness ran in him, as when the Puerto Rican elevator man sent him to the service entrance: but then it ebbed, and he admonished himself that Lushinski was his superior in rank and in years, a man the Prime Minister said had a heart like a root of a tree in his own back yard. This was a saying derived from the Dt' proverb: the man whose heart is rooted in his own garden will betray your garden, but the man whose heart is rooted in your garden will take care of it as if it were his own. (In the beautiful compressed idiom of the Prime Minister's middle-region argot: *bl'kt pk'ralwa, bl'kt duwam pk'ralwi.*)

And so instead of allowing himself to cultivate the hard little knob of jealousy that lived inside his neck, in the very spot where he swallowed food and drink, Morris reminded himself of his patriotism—his dear little country, still more a concept than a real nation, a confederacy of vast and enviously competitive families, his own prestigious tribe the most prominent, its females renowned for having the sleekest skin, even grandmothers' flesh smooth and tight as the flesh of panthers. He considered how inventiveness and adaptability marked his father and all his father's brothers, how on the tribe-god's day all the other families had to bring his great-uncle baskets of bean-flour and garlic buds, how on that day his great-uncle took out the tall tribe-god from its locked hut, and wreathed a garland of mallows on its *lulu*, and the females were shut into the tribe-god's stockade, and how at the first star of night the songs from the females behind the wall heated the sky and every boy of fourteen had his new bronze collar hitched on, and then how, wearing his collar, Morris led out of the god's stockade and into the shuddering forest his first female of his own, one of the aunties' young cousins, a pliant little girl of eleven....

In New York there were dangerous houses, it was necessary to be married to be respectable, not to acquire a disease, in New York it was not possible for an important young man to have a female of his own who was not his wife; in London it was rather more possible, he had gone often to the bedsitter of Isabel Oxenham, a cheerful, bony, homely young woman who explained that being a Cockney meant you were born within the sound of Bow Bells and therefore she was a Cockney, but in New York there was prejudice, it was more difficult, in this Lushinski could not be his model. . . . Now he was almost listening to the Secretary, and oh, he had conquered jealousy, he was proud that his country, so tender, so wise, so full of feeling, could claim a mind like Lushinski's to represent it! It was not a foreign mind, it was a mind like his own, elevated and polished. He heard the Secretary say "universal," and it occurred to him that the conversation had turned philosophical. Instantly he made a contribution to it; he was certain that philosophy and poetry were his only real interests: his strengths.

"At bottom," Morris said, "there is no contradiction between the tribal and the universal. Remember William Blake, sir: 'To see a world in a grain of sand'—"

The Secretary had white hair and an old, creased face; Morris loathed the slender purple veins that made flower-patterns along the sides of his nose. The ugliness, the defectiveness, of some human beings! God must have had a plan for them if He created them, but since one did not understand the plan, one could not withhold one's loathing. It was not a moral loathing, it was only aesthetic. "Nationalism," Morris said, "in the West is so very recent: a nineteenth-century development. But in Africa we have never had that sort of thing. Our notion of nationhood is different, it has nothing political attached to it; it is for the dear land itself, the customs, the rites, the cousins, the sense of family. A sense of family gives one a more sublime concept: one is readier to think of the Human Family," but he thanked his mother that he was not related to this old, carmine-colored, creased and ugly man.

On the way back to New York in the shuttle plane Lushinski spoke to him like a teacher—avoiding English, so as not to be overheard. "That man is a peasant," he told Morris. "It is never necessary to make conversation with peasants. They are like their own dogs or pigs or donkeys. They only know if it rains. They look out only for their own corner. He will make us starve if we let him." And he said, using the middle-region argot of the Prime Minister, "Let him eat air," which was, in that place, a dark curse, but one that always brought laughter. In spite of this, and in spite of the funny way he pronounced *hl'tk*, "starve," aspirating it (*hlt'k*) instead of churning it in his throat, so that it came out a sort of half-pun for "take-away-the-virginity-of," Morris noticed again that whenever Lushinski said the word "peasant" he looked afraid. The war, of course, happened. For a week the cables flew. Lushinski flew too, to consult with the Prime Minister; he had letters from the Secretary, which he took with him to burn in the Prime Minister's ashtray. Morris remained in New York. One evening Lulu telephoned, to invite him to supper. He heard in her voice that she was obeying her lover, so he declined.

The war was more than fifty miles north of the capital. The Prime Minister's bungalow was beaten by rain; after the rain, blasts of hot wind shook the shutters. The leaves, which had been turned into cups and wells, dried instantly. Evaporation everywhere sent up steam and threads of rainbows. The air-conditioners rattled like tin pans. One by one Lushinski tore up the Secretary's letters, kindling them in the Prime Minister's ashtray with the Prime Minister's cigarette lighter—it was in the shape of the Leaning Tower of Pisa. Then he stoked them in the Prime Minister's ashtray with the Prime Minister's Japanese-made fountain pen. Even indoors, even with the air-conditioners grinding away, the sunlight was dense with scents unknown in New York: rubber mingled with straw and tar and monkey-droppings and always the drifting smell of the mimosas. The Prime Minister's wife (he pretended to be monogamous, though he had left off using this one long ago)—rather, the female who had the status of the Prime Minister's wife—went on her knees to Lushinski and presented him with a sacerdotal bean-flour cake.

The war lasted a second week; when the Prime Minister signed the cease-fire, Lushinski stood at his side, wearing no expression at all. From the Secretary came a congratulatory cable; Lushinski read it under those perfumed trees, heavy as cabbage-heads, smoking and smoking—he was addicted to the local tobacco. His flesh drank the sun. The hills, rounder and greener than any other on the planet, made his chest blaze. From the airplane—now he was leaving Africa again—he imagined he saw the tarred roofs of the guerrilla camps in the shadows of the hills; or perhaps those were only the dark nests of vultures. They ascended, and through the window he fixed on the huge silver horn of the jet, and under it the white cloud-meadows.

In New York the Secretary praised him and called him a peacemaker. Privately Lushinski did not so much as twitch, but he watched Morris smile. They had given the Secretary air to eat! A month after the "war"—the quotation marks were visible in Lushinski's enunciation: what was it but a combination of village riots and semistrikes? only two hundred or so people killed, one of them unfortunately the Dt' poet L'duy—the price of the indispensable cuttings rose sixty per cent, increasing gross national income by two thirds. The land was like a mother whose breasts overflow. This was Morris's image: but Lushinski said, "She has expensive nipples, our mother." And then Morris understood that Lushinski had made the war the way a man in his sleep makes a genital dream, and that the Prime Minister had transfigured the dream into wet blood.

The Prime Minister ordered a bronze monument to commemorate the dead poet. Along the base were the lines, both in argot and in English,

The deer intends,	*Kt'ratalwo*
The lion fulfills.	*Mnep g'trpa*
Man the hunter	*Kt'bl ngaya wiba*
Only chooses sides.	*Gagl gagl mrpa.*

The translation into English was Lushinski's. Morris said worshipfully, "Ah, there is no one like you," and Lulu said, "How terrible to make a war just to raise prices," and Lushinski said, "For this there are many precedents."

To Morris he explained: "The war would have come in any case. It was necessary to adjust the timing. The adjustment saved lives"—here he set forth the preemptive strategy of the Rundabi, and how it was foiled: his mouth looked sly, he loved tricks—"and simultaneously it accomplished our needs. Remember this for when you are Ambassador. Don't try to ram against the inevitable. Instead, tinker with the timing." Though it was after midnight and they were alone in Morris's office—Lushinski's was too grand for unofficial conversation—they spoke in argot. Lushinski was thirstily downing a can of Coca-Cola and Morris was eating salted crackers spread with apple butter. "Will I be Ambassador?" Morris asked. "One day," Lushinski said, "the mother will throw me out." Morris did not understand. "The motherland? Never!" "The mother," Lushinski corrected, "Tanake-Tuka." "Oh, never!" cried Morris, "you bring her luck." "I am not a totem," Lushinski said. But Morris pondered. "We civilized men," he said (using for "men" the formal term "lords," so that his thought ascended, he turned eloquent), "we do not comprehend what the more passionate primitive means when he says 'totem.' " "I am not afraid of words," Lushinski said. "You are," Morris said.

Lulu, like Morris, had also noticed a word which made Lushinski afraid. But she distinguished intelligently between bad memories and bad moods. He told her he was the century's one free man. She scoffed at such foolery. "Well, not the only one," he conceded. "But more free than most. Every survivor is free. Everything that can happen to a human being has already happened inside the survivor. The future can invent nothing worse. What he owns now is recklessness without fear."

This was his diplomat's English. Lulu hated it. "You didn't die," she said. "Don't be pompous about being alive. If you were dead like the others, you would have something to be pompous about. People call them martyrs, and they were only ordinary. If you were a martyr, you could preen about it."

"Do you think me ordinary?" he asked. He looked just then like a crazy man burning with a secret will; but this was nothing, he could make himself look any way he pleased. "If I were ordinary I would be dead."

She could not deny this. A child strung of sticks, he had survived the peasants who baited and blistered and beat and hunted him. One of them had hanged him from the rafter of a shed, by the wrists. He was four sticks hanging. And his stomach shrank and shrank, and now it was inelastic, still the size of a boy's stomach, and he could not eat. She brought him a bowl of warm farina, and watched him push the spoon several times into the straight line of his mouth;

then he put away the spoon; then she took his head down into her lap, as if it were the head of a doll, and needed her own thoughts to give it heat.

He offered her books.

"Why should I read all this? I'm not curious about history, only about you."

"One and the same," he said.

"Pompous," she told him again. He allowed her only this one subject. "Death," she said. "Death, death, death. What do you care? *You* came out alive." "I care about the record," he insisted. There were easy books and there were hard books. The easier ones were stories; these she brought home herself. But they made him angry. "No stories, no tales," he said. "Sources. Documents only. Politics. This is what led to my profession. Accretion of data. There are no holy men of stories," he said, "there are only holy men of data. Remember this before you fall at the feet of anyone who makes romances out of what really happened. If you want something liturgical, say to yourself: *what really happened.*" He crashed down on the bed beside her an enormous volume: it was called *The Destruction.* She opened it and saw tables and figures and asterisks; she saw train-schedules. It was all dry, dry. "Do you know that writer?" she asked; she was accustomed to his being acquainted with everyone. "Yes," he said, "do you want to have dinner with him?" "No," she said.

She read the stories and wept. She wept over the camps. She read a book called *Night*; she wept. "But I can't separate all that," she pleaded, "the stories and the sources."

"Imagination is romance. Romance blurs. Instead count the numbers of freight trains."

She read a little in the enormous book. The title irritated her. It was a lie. "It isn't as if the whole *world* was wiped out. It wasn't like the Flood. It wasn't *mankind*, after all, it was only one population. The Jews aren't the whole world, they aren't mankind, are they?"

She caught in his face a prolonged strangeness: he was new to her, like someone she had never looked at before. "What's the matter, Stasek?" But all at once she saw: she had said he was not mankind.

"Whenever people remember mankind," he said, "they don't fail to omit the Jews."

"An epigram!" she threw out. "What's the good of an epigram! Self-conscious! In public you make jokes, but at home—"

"At home I make water," and went into the bathroom.

"Stasek?" she said through the door.

"You'd better go read."

"Why do you want me to know all that?"

"To show you what you're living with."

"I know who I'm living with!"

"I didn't say *who*, I said *what*."

The shower water began.

She shouted, "You always want a bath whenever I say that word!"

"Baptism," he called. "Which word? Mankind?"

"Stasek!" She shook the knob; he had turned the lock. "Listen, Stasek, I want to tell you something. Stasek! I want to say something *important*."

He opened the door. He was naked. "Do you know what's important?" he asked her.

She fixed on his member; it was swollen. She announced, "I want to tell you what I hate."

"I hope it's not what you're staring at," he said.

"History," she said. "History's what I hate."

"Poor Lulu, some of it got stuck on you and it won't come off—"

"Stasek!"

"Come wash it away, we'll have a tandem baptism."

"I know what *you* hate," she accused. "You hate being part of the Jews. You hate that."

"I am not part of the Jews. I am part of mankind. You're not going to say they're the same thing?"

She stood and reflected. She was sick of his satire. She felt vacuous and ignorant. "Practically nobody knows you're a Jew," she said. "*I* never think of it. You always make me think of it. If I forget it for a while you give me a book, you make me read history, three wars ago, as remote as Attila the Hun. And then I say that word"—she breathed, she made an effort—"I say *Jew*, and you run the water, you get afraid. And then when you get afraid you *attack*, it all comes back on you, you attack like an animal—"

Out of the darkness came the illusion of his smile: oh, a sun! She saw him beautifully beaming. "If not for history," he said, "think! You'd still be in the *Schloss*, you wouldn't have become a little American girl, you wouldn't have grown up to the lipstick factory—"

"Did you leave the drain closed?" she said suddenly. "Stasek, with the shower going, how stupid, now look, the tub's almost ready to overflow—"

He smiled and smiled: "Practically nobody knows you're a princess."

"I'm *not*. It's my great-aunt—oh for God's sake, there it goes, over the side." She peeled off her shoes and went barefoot into the flood and reached to shut off the water. Her feet streamed, her two hands streamed. Then she faced him. "Princess! I know what it is with you! The more you mock, the more you mean it, but I know what it is! You want little stories, deep gossip, you want to pump me and pump me, you have a dream of royalty, and you know perfectly well,

you've known it from the first *minute*, I've told and told how
I spent the whole of the war in school in England! And then
you say nonsense like 'little American girl' because you want
that too, you want a princess and you want America and you
want Europe and you want Africa—"

But he intervened. "I don't want Europe," he said.

"Pompous! Mockery! You want everything you're not,
that's what it's about! Because of what you are!" She let
herself laugh; she fell into laughter like one of his audiences.
"An African! An African!"

"Louisa"—he had a different emphasis now: "I am an
African," and in such a voice, all the sinister gaming out of
it, the voice of a believer. Did he in truth believe in Africa?
He did not take her there. Pictures swam in her of what it
might be—herons, plumage, a red stalk of bird-leg in an un-
moving pool, mahogany nakedness and golden collars, drums,
black bodies, the women with their hooped lips, loin-strings,
yellow fur stalking, dappled, striped . . . the fear, the fear.

He pushed his nakedness against her. Her hand was wet.
Always he was cold to Jews. He never went among them. In
the Assembly he turned his back on the ambassador from
Israel; she was in the reserved seats, she saw it herself, she
heard the gallery gasp. All New York Jews in the gallery.
She knew the word he was afraid of. He pressed her, he
made himself her master, she read what he gave her, she,
once securely her own mistress, who now followed when he
instructed and stayed when he ordered it, she knew when
to make him afraid.

"You Jew," she said.

Without words he had told her when to say those words;
she was obedient and restored him to fear.

· · ·

Morris, despite his classical education, had no taste for
Europe. No matter that he had studied "political science"—
he turned it all into poetry, or, at the least, psychology;
better yet, gossip. He might read a biography but he did not
care about the consequences of any life. He remembered the
names of Princess Margaret's dogs and it seemed to him that
Hitler, though unluckily mad, was a genius, because he saw
how to make a whole people search for ecstasy. Morris did
not understand Europe. Nevertheless he knew he was superior to Europe, as people who are accustomed to a stable
temperature are always superior to those who must live with
the zaniness of the seasons. His reveries were attuned to a
steady climate—summer, summer. In his marrow the crick-
ets were always rioting, the mantises always flashing: sometimes a mantis stood on a leaf and put its two front legs one
over the other, like a good child.

Lushinski seemed to him invincibly European: Africa
was all light, all fine scent, sweet deep rain and again light,
brilliance, the cleansing heat of shining. And Europe by con-
trast a coal, hellish and horrible, even the snows dark because humped and shadowy, caves, paw-prints of wolves,
shoe-troughs of fleeing. In Africa you ran for joy, the joyous
thighs begged for fleetness, you ran into veld and bush and
green. In Europe you fled, it was flight, you ran like prey
into shadows: Europe the Dark Continent.

Under klieg lights Lushinski grew more and more polished; he was becoming a comic artist, he learned when to
stop for water, when to keep the tail of a phrase in abeyance.
Because of television he was invited to talk everywhere. His
stories were grotesque, but he told them so plausibly that he
outraged everyone into nervous howls. People liked him to
describe his student days in Moscow, after the Russian soldiers had liberated him; they liked him to tell about his
suitcase, about his uniform.

He gave very little. He was always very brief. But they laughed. "In Moscow," he said, "we lived five in one room. It had once been the servant's room of a large elegant house. Twenty-seven persons, male and female, shared the toilet; but we in our room were lucky because we had a balcony. One day I went out on the balcony to build a bookcase for the room. I had some boards for shelves and a tin of nails and a hammer and a saw, and I began banging away. And suddenly one of the other students came flying out onto the balcony: 'People at the door! People at the door!' There were mobs of callers out there, ringing, knocking, yelling. That afternoon I received forty-six orders in three hours, for a table, a credenza, endless bookshelves, a bed, a desk, a portable commode. They thought I was an illegal carpenter working out in the open that way to advertise: you had to wait months for a State carpenter. One of the orders—it was for the commode—was from an informer. I explained that I was only a student and not in business, but they locked me up for hooliganism because I had drawn a crowd. Five days in a cell with drunkards. They said I had organized a demonstration against the regime.

"A little while afterward the plumbing of our communal toilet became defective—I will not say just how. The solid refuse had to be gathered in buckets. It was unbearable, worse than any stable. And again I saw my opportunity as a carpenter. I constructed a commode and delivered it to the informer—and oh, it was full, it was full. Twenty-seven Soviet citizens paid tribute."

Such a story made Morris uncomfortable. His underwear felt too tight, he perspired. He wondered why everyone laughed. The story seemed to him European, uncivilized. It was something that could have happened but probably did not happen. He did not know what he ought to believe.

The suitcase, on the other hand, he knew well. It was

always reliably present, leaning against Lushinksi's foot, or propped up against the bottom of his desk, or the door of his official car. Lushinski was willing enough to explain its contents: "Several complete sets of false papers," he said with satisfaction, looking the opposite of sly, and one day he displayed them. There were passports for various identities—English, French, Brazilian, Norwegian, Dutch, Australian—and a number of diplomas in different languages. "The two Russian ones," he boasted, "aren't forgeries," putting everything back among new shirts still in their wrappers.

"But why, why?" Morris said.

"A maxim. Always have your bags packed."

"But why?"

"To get away."

"Why?"

"Sometimes it's better where you aren't than where you are."

Morris wished the Prime Minister had heard this; surely he would have trusted Lushinski less. But Lushinski guessed his thought. "Only the traitors stay home," he said. "In times of trouble only the patriots have false papers."

"But now the whole world knows," Morris said reasonably. "You've told the whole world on television."

"That will make it easier to get away. They will recognize a patriot and defer."

He became a dervish of travel: he was mad about America and went to Detroit and to Tampa, to Cincinnati and to Biloxi. They asked him how he managed to keep up with his diplomatic duties; he referred them to Morris, whom he called his "conscientious blackamoor." Letters came to the consulate in New York accusing him of being a colonialist and a racist. Lushinski remarked that he was not so much that as a cyclist, and immediately—to prove his solidarity

with cyclists of every color—bought Morris a gleaming ten-
speed two-wheeler. Morris had learned to ride at Oxford,
and was overjoyed once again to pedal into a rush of wind.
He rode south on Second Avenue; he circled the whole
Lower East Side. But in only two days his bike was stolen
by a gang of what the police designated as "teen-age black
male perpetrators." Morris liked America less and less.

Lushinski liked it more and more. He went to civic clubs,
clubs with animal names, clubs with Indian names; societies
internationalist and jingoist; veterans, pacifists, vegetarians,
feminists, vivisectionists; he would agree to speak anywhere.
No Jews invited him; he had turned his back on the Israeli
ambassador. Meanwhile the Secretary of State withdrew a
little, and omitted Lushinski from his dinner list; he was
repelled by a man who would want to go to Cincinnati, a
place the Secretary had left forever. But the Prime Minister
was delighted and cabled Lushinski to "get to know the
proletariat"—nowadays the Prime Minister often used such
language: he said "dialectic," "collective," and "Third
World." Occasionally he said "peoples," as in "peoples' republic." In a place called Oneonta, New York, Lushinski told
about the uniform: in Paris he had gone to a tailor and asked
him to make up the costume of an officer. "Of which nation-
ality, sir?" "Oh, no particular one." "What rank, sir?" "High.
As high as you can imagine." The coat was long, had
epaulets, several golden bands on the sleeves, and metal but-
tons engraved with the head of a dead monarch. From a toy
store Lushinski bought ribbons and medals to hang on its
breast. The cap was tall and fearsomely military, with a
strong bill ringed by a scarlet cord. Wearing this concoction,
Lushinski journeyed to the Rhineland. In hotels they gave
him the ducal suite and charged nothing, in restaurants he
swept past everyone to the most devoted service, at airports

he was served drinks in carpeted sitting rooms and ushered on board, with a guard, into a curtained parlor.

"Your own position commands all that," Morris said gravely. Again he was puzzled. All around him they rattled with hilarity. Lushinski's straight mouth remained straight; Morris brooded about impersonation. It was no joke (but this was years and years ago, in the company of Isabel Oxenham) that he sought out Tarzan movies: Africa in the Mind of the West. It could have been his thesis, but it was not. He was too inward for such a generality: it was his own mind he meant to observe. Was he no better than that lout Tarzan, investing himself with a chatter not his own? How long could the ingested, the invented, foreignness endure? He felt himself—himself, Mdulgo-kt'dulgo, called Morris, dressed in suit and tie, his academic gown thrown down on a chair twenty miles north of this cinema—he felt himself to be self-duped, an impersonator. The film passed (jungle, vines, apes, the famous leap and screech and fisted thump, natives each with his rubber spear and extra's face—janitors and barmen), it was a confusion, a mist. His thumb climbed Isabel's vertebrae: such a nice even row, up and down like a stair. The children's matinee was done, the evening film commenced. It was in Italian, and he never forgot it, a comedy about an unwilling impostor, a common criminal mistaken for a heroic soldier: General della Rovere.

The movie made Isabel's tears fall onto Morris's left wrist.

The criminal, an ordinary thug, is jailed; the General's political enemies want the General put away. The real General is a remarkable man, a saint, a hero. And, little by little, the criminal acquires the General's qualities, he becomes selfless, he becomes courageous, glorious. At the end of the movie he has a chance to reveal that he is not the real General della Rovere. Nobly, he chooses instead to be executed in the General's place, he atones for his past life, a voluntary sacrifice. Morris explained to Isabel that the ferocious natives encountered by Tarzan are in the same moral situation as the false General della Rovere: they accommodate, they adapt to what is expected. Asked to howl like men who inhabit no culture, they howl. "But they have souls, once they were advanced beings. If you jump into someone else's skin," he asked, "doesn't it begin to fit you?"

"Oi wouldn now, oi hev no ejucytion," Isabel said.

Morris himself did not know.

All the same, he did not believe that Lushinski was this sort of impersonator. A Tarzan perhaps, not a della Rovere. The problem of sincerity disturbed and engrossed him. He boldly asked Lushinski his views.

"People who deal in diplomacy attach too much importance to being believed," Lushinski declaimed. "Sincerity is only a maneuver, like any other. A quantity of lies is a much more sensible method—it gives the effect of greater choice. Sincerity offers only one course. But if you select among a great variety of insincerities, you're bound to strike a better course."

He said all this because it was exactly what Morris wanted to hear from him.

The Prime Minister had no interest in questions of identity. "He is not a false African," the Prime Minister said in a parliamentary speech defending his appointment, "he is a true advocate." Though vainglorious, this seemed plausible enough; but for Morris, Lushinski was not an African at all. "It isn't enough to be *politically* African," Morris argued one night; "politically you can assume the culture. No one can assume the cult." Then he remembered the little bones of Isabel Oxenham's back. "Morris, Morris," Lushinski said, "you're not beginning to preach Negritude?" "No," said Morris; he wanted to speak of religion, of his mother; but just then he could not—the telephone broke in, though it was one in the morning and not the official number, rather his own private one, used by Louisa. She spoke of returning to her profession; she was too often alone. "Where are you going tomorrow?" she asked Lushinski. Morris could hear the little electric voice in the receiver. "You say you do it for public relations," she said, "but why really? What do they need to know about Africa in Shaker Heights that they don't know already?" The little electric voice forked and fragmented, tiny lightnings in her lover's ear.

The next day a terrorist from one of the hidden guerrilla camps in the hills shot the Prime Minister's wife at a government ceremony with many Westerners present; he had intended to shoot the Prime Minister. The Prime Minister, it was noted, appeared to grieve, and ordered a bubble-top for his car and a bulletproof vest to wear under his shirt. In a cable he instructed Lushinski to cease his circulation among the American proletariat. Lulu was pleased. Lushinski began to refuse invitations, his American career was over. In the Assembly he spoke—"with supernal," Morris acknowledged, "eloquence"—against terrorism; though their countries had no diplomatic relations, and in spite of Lushinski's public snub, the Israeli ambassador applauded, with liquid eyes. But Lushinski missed something. To address an international body representing every nation on the planet seemed less than before; seemed limiting; he missed the laughter of Oneonta, New York. The American provinces moved him—how gullible they were, how little they knew, or would ever know, of cruelty's breadth! A country of babies. His half-year among all those cities had elated him: a visit to an innocent star: no sarcasm, cynicism, innuendo grew there; such nice church ladies; a benevolent passiveness which his tales, with their wily spikes, could rouse to nervous pleasure.

Behind Lushinski's ears threads of white hairs sprang; he worried about the Prime Minister's stability in the aftermath of the attack. While the representative from Uganda "exercised," Lushinski sneered, "his right of reply"—"The distinguished representative from our sister-country to the north fabricates dangerous adventures for make-believe pirates who exist only in his fantasies, and we all know how colorfully, how excessively, he is given to whimsy"—Lushinski drew on his pad the head of a cormorant, with a sack under its beak. Though there was no overt resemblance, it could pass nevertheless for a self-portrait.

In October he returned to his capital. The Prime Minister had a new public wife. He had replenished his ebullience, and no longer wore the bulletproof vest. The new wife kneeled before Lushinski with a bean-flour cake. The Prime Minister was sanguine: the captured terrorist had informed on his colleagues, entire nests of them had been cleaned out of four nearby villages. The Prime Minister begged Lushinski to allow him to lend him one of his younger females. Lushinski examined her and accepted. He took also one of Morris's sisters, and with these two went to live for a month alone in a white villa on the blue coast.

Every day the Prime Minister sent a courier with documents and newspapers; also the consular pouch from New York.

Morris in New York: Morris in a city of Jews. He walked. He crossed a bridge. He walked. He was attentive to their houses, their neighborhoods. Their religious schools. Their synagogues. Their multitudinous societies. Announcements of debates, ice cream, speeches, rallies, delicatessens, violins, felafel, books. Ah, the avalanche of their books!

Where their streets ended, the streets of the blacks began. Mdulgo-kt'dulgo in exile among the kidnapped—cargo-Africans, victims with African faces, lost to language and faith; impostors sunk in barbarism, primitives, impersonators. Emptied-out creatures, with their hidden knives, their swift silver guns, their poisoned red eyes, christianized, made not new but neuter, fabricated: oh, only restore them to their inmost selves, to the serenity of orthodoxy, redemption of the true gods who speak in them without voice!

Morris Ngambe in New York. Alone, treading among traps, in jeopardy of ambush, with no female.

And in Africa, in a white villa on the blue coast: the Prime Minister's gaudy pet, on a blue sofa before an open window, smoking and smoking, under the breath of the scented trees, under the sleek palms of a pair of young females, smoking and caressing—snug in Africa, Lushinski.

In Lushinski's last week in the villa, the pouch from New York held a letter from Morris.

The letter:

A curious note concerning the terrorist personality. I have just read of an incident which took place in a Jerusalem prison. A captive terrorist, a Japanese who had murdered twenty-nine pilgrims at the Tel Aviv airport, was permitted to keep in his cell, besides reading matter, a comb, a hairbrush, a nailbrush, and a fingernail clippers. A dapper chap, apparently. One morning he was found to have partially circumcised himself. His instrument was the clippers. He lost consciousness and the job was completed in the prison hospital. The doctor questioned him. It turned out he had begun to read intensively in the Jewish religion. He had a Bible and a text for learning the Hebrew language. He had begun to grow a beard and earlocks. Perhaps you will understand better than I the spiritual side of this matter.

You recall my remarks on culture and cult. Here is a man who wishes to annihilate a society and its culture, but he is captivated by its cult. For its cult he will bleed himself.

Captivity leading to captivation: an interesting notion.

It may be that every man at length becomes what he wishes to victimize.

It may be that every man needs to impersonate what he first must kill.

Lushinski recognized in Morris's musings a lumpy parroting of *Reading Gaol* mixed with—what? Fanon? Genet? No; only Oscar Wilde, sentimentally epigrammatic. Oscar Wilde in Jerusalem! As unlikely as the remorse of Gomorrah. Like everyone the British had once blessed with Empire, Morris was a Victorian. He was a gentleman. He believed in civilizing influences; even more in civility. He was besotted by style. If he thought of knives, it was for buttering scones.

But Lushinski, a man with the nose and mouth of a knife, and the body of a knife, understood this letter as a blade between them. It meant a severing. Morris saw him as an impersonator. Morris uncovered him; then stabbed. Morris had called him a transmuted, a transfigured, African. A man in love with his cell. A traitor. Perfidious. A fake.

Morris had called him Jew.

—Morris in New York, alone, treading among traps, in jeopardy of ambush, with no female. He knew his ascendancy. Victory of that bird-bright forest, glistening with the bodies of boys, over the old terror in the Polish woods.

Morris prayed. He prayed to his mother: down, take him down, bring him something evil. The divine mother answers sincere believers: O Tanake-Tuka!

And in Africa, in a white villa on the blue coast, the Prime Minister's gaudy pet, on a blue sofa before an open window, smoking and smoking, under the breath of the scented trees, under the shadow of the bluish snow, under the blue-black pillars of the Polish woods, under the breath of Andor, under the merciless palms of peasants and fists of peasants, under the rafters, under the stone-white hanging stars of Poland—Lushinski.

Against the stones and under the snow.

(*1974*)

Bloodshed

Bleilip took a Greyhound bus out of New York and rode through icy scenes half-urban and half-countrified until he arrived at the town of the hasidim. He had intended to walk, but his coat pockets were heavy, so he entered a loitering taxi. Though it was early on a Sunday afternoon he saw no children at all. Then he remembered that they would be in the yeshivas until the darker slant of the day. Yeshivas not yeshiva: small as the community was, it had three or four schools, and still others, separate, for the little girls. Toby and Yussel were waiting for him and waved his taxi down the lumpy road above their half-built house— it was a new town, and everything in it was new or promised: pavements, trash cans, septic tanks, newspaper stores. But just because everything was unfinished, you could sniff raw-ness, the opened earth meaty and scratched up as if by big animal claws, the frozen puddles in the basins of ditches fresh-smelling, mossy.

Toby he regarded as a convert. She was just barely a relative, a third or fourth cousin, depending on how you counted, whether from his mother or from his father, who were also cousins to each other. She came from an ordinary family, not especially known for its venturesomeness, but now she looked to him altogether uncommon, freakish: her bun was a hairpiece pinned on, over it she wore a bandanna (a *tcheptichke*, she called it), her sleeves stopped below her wrists, her dress was outlandishly long. With her large red face over this costume she almost passed for some sort of peasant. Though still self-reliant, she had become like all their women.

She served him orange juice. Bleilip, feeling his bare bald head, wondered whether he was expected to say the blessing, whether they would thrust a headcovering on him: he was baffled, confused, but Yussel said, "You live your life and I'll live mine, do what you like," so he drank it all down quickly. Relief made him thirsty, and he drank more and more from a big can with pictures of sweating oranges on it—some things they bought at a supermarket like all mortals.

"So," he said to Toby, "how do you like your *shtetl?*"

She laughed and circled a finger around at the new refrigerator, vast-shouldered, gleaming, a presence. "What a village we are! A backwater!"

"State of mind," he said, "that's what I meant."

"Oh, state of mind. What's that?"

"Everything here feels different," was all he could say.

"We're in pieces, that's why. When the back rooms are put together we'll seem more like a regular house."

"The carpenter," Yussel said, "works only six months a year—we got started with him a month before he stopped. So we have to wait."

"What does he do the rest of the year?"

"He teaches."

"He teaches?"

"He trades with Shmulka Gershons. The other half of the year Shmulka Gershons lays pipes. Six months *Gemara* with the boys, six months on the job. Mr. Horowitz the carpenter also."

Bleilip said uncertainly, meaning to flatter, "It sounds like a wonderful system."

"It's not a *system,*" Yussel said.

"Yussel goes everywhere, a commuter," Toby said: Yussel was a salesman for a paper-box manufacturer. He wore a small trimmed beard, very black, black-rimmed eyeglasses, and a vest over a rounding belly. Bleilip saw that Yussel liked him—he led him away from Toby and showed him the new hot air furnace in the cellar, the gas-fired hot water tank, the cinder blocks piled in the yard, the deep cuts above the road where the sewer pipes would go. He pointed over a little wooded crest—they could just see a bit of unpainted roof. "That's our yeshiva, the one our boys go to. It's not the toughest, they're not up to it. They weren't good enough. In the other yeshiva in the city they didn't give them enough work. Here," he said proudly, "they go from seven till half-past six."

They went back into the house by the rear door. Bleilip believed in instant rapport and yearned for closeness—he wanted to be close, close. But Yussel was impersonal, a guide, he froze Bleilip's vision. They passed through the bedrooms and again it seemed to Bleilip that Yussel was a real estate agent, a bureaucrat, a tourist office. There were a few shelves of books—holy books, nothing frivolous—but no pictures on the walls, no radio anywhere, no television set. Bleilip had brought with him, half-furtively, a snapshot of Toby taken eight or nine years before: Toby squatting on the grass at Brooklyn College, short curly hair with a barrette glinting in it, high socks and loafers, glimpse of panties, wispy blouse blurred by wind, a book with its title clear to the camera: Political Science. He offered this to Yussel: "A classmate." Yussel looked at the wall. "Why do I need an image? I have my wife right in front of me every morning." Toby held the wallet, saw, smiled, gave it back. "Another life," she said.

Bleilip reminded her, "The joke was which would be the

bigger breakthrough, the woman or the Jew—" To Yussel he explained, "She used to say she would be the first lady Jewish President."

"Another life, other jokes," Toby said.

"And this life? Do you like it so much?"

"Why do you keep asking? Don't you like your own life?"

Bleilip liked his life, he liked it excessively. He felt he was part of society-at-large. He told her, without understanding why he was saying such a thing, "Here there's nothing to mock at, no jokes."

"You said we're a village," she contradicted.

"That wasn't mockery."

"It wasn't, you meant it. You think we're fanatics, primitives."

"Leave the man be," Yussel said. He had a cashier's tone, guide counting up the day's take, and Bleilip was grieved, because Yussel was a survivor, everyone in the new town, except one or two oddities like Toby, was a survivor of the deathcamps or the child of a survivor. "He's looking for something. He wants to find. He's not the first and he won't be the last." The rigid truth of this—Bleilip had thought his purposes darkly hidden—shocked him. He hated accuracy in a survivor. It was an affront. He wanted some kind of haze, a nostalgia for suffering perhaps. He resented the orange juice can, the appliances, the furnace, the sewer pipes. "He's been led to expect saints," Yussel said. "Listen, Jules," he said, "I'm not a saint and Toby's not a saint and we don't have miracles and we don't have a rebbe who works miracles."

"You have a rebbe," Bleilip said; instantly a wash of blood filled his head.

"He can't fly. What we came here for was to live a life of study. Our own way, and not to be interrupted in it."

"For the man, not the woman. You, not Toby. Toby used to be smart. Achievement goals and so forth."

"Give the mother of four sons a little credit too, it's not only college girls who build the world," Yussel said in a voice so fair-minded and humorous and obtuse that Bleilip wanted to knock him down—the first lady Jewish President of the United States had succumbed in her junior year to the zealot's private pieties, rites, idiosyncrasies. Toby was less than lucid, she was crazy to follow deviants, not in the mainstream even of their own tradition. Bleilip, who had read a little, considered these hasidim actually christologized: everything had to go through a mediator. Of their popular romantic literature he knew the usual bits and pieces, legends, occult passions, quirks, histories—he had heard, for instance, about the holiday the Lubavitcher hasidim celebrate on the anniversary of their master's release from prison: pretty stories in the telling, even more touching in the reading—poetry. Bleilip, a lawyer though not in practice, an ex-labor consultant, a fund-raiser by profession, a rationalist, a *mitnagid* (he scarcely knew the word), purist, skeptic, enemy of fresh revelation, enemy of the hasidim!—repelled by the sects themselves, he was nevertheless lured by their constituents. Refugees, survivors. He supposed they had a certain knowledge the unscathed could not guess at.

He said: "Toby makes her bed, she lies in it. I didn't come expecting women's rights and God knows I didn't come expecting saints."

"If not saints then martyrs," Yussel said.

Bleilip said nothing. This was not the sort of closeness he coveted—he shunned being seen into. His intention was to be a benefactor of the feelings. He glimpsed Yussel's tattoo-number (it almost seemed as if Yussel just then lifted his wrist to display it) without the compassion he had schemed for it. He had come to see a town of dead men. It spoiled Bleilip's mood that Yussel understood this.

At dusk the three of them went up to the road to watch the boys slide down the hill from the yeshiva. There was no danger: not a single car, except Bleilip's taxi, had passed through all day. The snow was a week old, it was coming on to March, the air struck like a bell-clapper, but Bleilip could smell through the cold something different from the smell of winter. Smoke of woodfire seeped into his throat from somewhere with a deep pineyness that moved him: he had a sense of farness, clarity, other lands, displaced seasons, the brooks of a village, a foreign bird piercing. The yeshiva boys came down on their shoe-soles, one foot in front of the other, lurching, falling, rolling. A pair of them tobogganed past on a garbage-can lid. The rest jostled, tumbled, squawked, their yarmulkas dropping from their heads into the snow like gumdrops, coins, black inkwells. Bleilip saw hoops of halos wheeling everywhere, and he saw their ear-curls leaping over their cheeks, and all at once he penetrated into what he took to be the truth of this place—the children whirling on the hillside were false children, made of no flesh, it was a crowd of ghosts coming down, a clamor of white smoke beat on the road. Yussel said, "I'm on my way to *mincha*, want to come?" Bleilip's grandfather, still a child but with an old man's pitted nose, appeared to be flying toward him on the lid. The last light of day split into blue rays all around them; the idea of going for evening prayer seemed natural to him now, but Bleilip, privately elated, self-proud, asked, "Why, do you need someone?"—because he was remembering what he had forgotten he knew. Ten men. He congratulated his memory, also of his grandfather's nose, thin as an arrow— the nose, the face, the body, all gone into the earth—and he

went on piecing together his grandfather's face, tan teeth
that gave out small clicks and radiated stale farina, shapely
gray half-moon eyes with fleshy lids, eyebrows sparse as a
woman's, a prickly whiskbroom of a mustache whiter than
cream. Yussel took him by the arm: "Pessimist, joker, here
we never run short, a *minyan* always without fail, but come,
anyhow you'll hear the rebbe, it's our turn for him." Briefly
behind them Bleilip saw Toby moving into the dark of the
door, trailed by two pairs of boys with golden earlocks: he
felt the shock of that sight, as if a beam of divinity had fixed
on her head, her house. But in an instant he was again humiliated by the sting of Yussel's eye—"She'll give them supper," he said merely, "then they have homework." "You people make them work." "Honey on the page is only for the
beginning," Yussel said, "afterward comes hard learning."

Bleilip accepted a cap for his cold-needled skull and they
toiled on the ice upward toward the schoolhouse: the rebbe
gave himself each week to a different *minyan*. When Bleilip
reached for a prayer-shawl inside a cardboard box Yussel
thumbed a No at him, so he dropped it in again. No one else
paid him any attention. Through the window the sky deep-
ened; the shouts were gone from the hill. Yussel handed him
a *sidur*, but the alphabet was jumpy and strange to him: it
needed piecing together, like his grandfather's visage. He
stood up when the others did. Then he sat down again, fit-
ting his haunches into a boy's chair. It did not seem to him
that they sang out with any special fervor, as he had read
the hasidim did, but the sounds were loud, cadenced, earnest. The leader, unlike the others a mutterer, was the single
one wearing the fringed shawl—it made a cave for him, he
looked out of it without mobility of heart. Bleilip turned his
stare here and there into the tedium—which was the rebbe?
He went after a politician's face: his analogy was to the

mayor of a town. Or a patriarch's face—the father of a large family. They finished *mincha* and herded themselves into a corner of the room—a long table (three planks nailed together, two sawhorses) covered by a cloth. The cloth was grimy: print lay on it, the backs of old *sidurim*, rubbing, shredding, the backs of the open hands of the men. Bleilip drew himself in; he found a wooden folding chair and wound his legs into the rungs, away from the men. It stunned him that they were not old, but instead mainly in the forties, plump and in their prime. Their cheeks were blooming hillocks above their beards; some wore yarmulkas, some tall black hats, some black hats edged with fur, some ordinary fedoras pushed back, one a workman's cap. Their mouths especially struck him as extraordinary—vigorous, tender, blessed. He marveled at their mouths until it came to him that they were speaking another language and that he could follow only a little of it: now and then it was almost as if their words were visibly springing out of their mouths, like flags or streamers. Whenever he understood the words the flags whipped at him, otherwise they collapsed and vanished with a sort of hum. Bleilip himself was a month short of forty-two, but next to these pious men he felt like a boy; even his shoulder-blades weakened and thinned. He made himself concentrate: he heard *azazel*, and he heard *kohen gadol*, they were knitting something up, mixing strands of holy tongue with Yiddish. The noise of Yiddish in his ear enfeebled him still more, like Titus's fly—it was not an everyday language with him, except to make cracks with, jokes, gags. . . . His dead grandfather hung from the ceiling on a rope. Wrong, mistaken, impossible, uncharacteristic of his grandfather!—who died old and safe in a Bronx bed, mischief-maker, eager aged imp. The imp came to life and swung over Bleilip's black corner. Here ghosts sat as if al-

ready in the World-to-Come, explicating Scripture. Or
whatever. Who knew? In his grandfather's garble the hasidim
(refugees, dead men) were crying out Temple, were crying
out High Priest, and the more Bleilip squeezed his brain
toward them, the more he comprehended. Five times on the
tenth day of the seventh month, the Day of Atonement, the
High Priest changes his vestments, five times he lowers his
body into the ritual bath. After the first immersion garments
of gold, after the second immersion white linen, and wearing
the white linen he confesses his sins and the sins of his
household while holding on to the horns of a bullock. Walk-
ing eastward, he goes from the west of the altar to the north
of the altar, where two goats stand, and he casts lots for the
goats: one for the Lord, one for Azazel, and the one for the
Lord is given a necklace of red wool and will be slaughtered
and its blood caught in a bowl, but first the bullock will be
slaughtered and its blood caught in a bowl; and once more he
confesses his sins and the sins of his household, and now also
the sins of the children of Aaron, this holy people. The blood
of the bullock is sprinkled eight times, both upward and downward, the blood of the goat is sprinkled eight times, then the
High Priest comes to the goat who was not slaughtered, the
one for Azazel, and now he touches it and confesses the sins
of the whole house of Israel, and utters the name of God,
and pronounces the people cleansed of sin. And Bleilip,
hearing all this through the web of a language gone stale in
his marrow, was scraped to the edge of pity and belief, he
pitied the hapless goats, the unlucky bullock, but more than
this he pitied the God of Israel, whom he saw as an imp with
a pitted nose dangling on a cord from the high beams of the
Temple in Jerusalem, winking down at His tiny High Priest
—now he leaps in and out of a box of water, now he hurries
in and out of new clothes like a quick-change vaudevillian,

now he sprinkles red drops up and red drops down, and all the while Bleilip, together with the God of the Jews, pities these toy children of Israel in the Temple long ago. Pity upon pity. What God could take the Temple rites seriously? What use does the King of the Universe have for goats? What, leaning on their dirty tablecloth—no vestments, altars, sacrifices—what do these survivors, exemptions, expect of God now?

All at once Bleilip knew which was the rebbe. The man in the work-cap, with a funny flat nose, black-haired and red-bearded, fist on mouth, elbows sunk into his lap—a self-stabber: in all that recitation, those calls and streamers of discourse, this blunt-nosed man had no word: but now he stood up, scratched his chair backward, and fell into an ordinary voice. Bleilip examined him: he looked fifty, his hands were brutish, two fingers missing, the nails on the others absent. A pair of muscles bunched in his neck like chains. The company did not breathe and gave him something more than attentiveness. Bleilip reversed his view and saw that the rebbe was their child, they gazed at him with the possessiveness of faces seized by a crib, and he too spoke in that mode, as if he were addressing parents, old fathers, deferential, awed, guilty. And still he was their child, and still he owed them his guilt. He said: "And what comes next? Next we read that the *kohen gadol* gives the goat fated for Azazel to one of the *kohanim*, and the *kohen* takes it out into a place all bare and wild, with a big cliff in the middle of it all, and he cuts off a bit of the red wool they had put on it, and ties it onto a piece of rock to mark the place, and then he drives the goat over the edge and it spins down, down, down, and is destroyed. But in the Temple the worship may not continue, not until it is known that the goat is already given over to the wilderness. How can they know this miles away in the far city? All along the way from the wilderness to Jerusalem, poles stand up out of the ground, and on top of every pole a man, and in the hand of every man a great shawl to shake out, so that pole flies out a wing to pole, wing after wing, until it comes to the notice of the *kohen gadol* in the Temple that the goat has been dashed into the ravine. And only then can the *kohen gadol* finish his readings, his invocations, his blessings, his beseechings. In the neighborhood of Sharon often there are earthquakes: the *kohen gadol* says: let their homes not become their graves. And after all this a procession, no, a parade, a celebration, all the people follow the *kohen gadol* to his own house, he is safe out of the Holy of Holies, their sins are atoned for, they are cleansed and healed, and they sing how like a flower he is, a lily, like the moon, the sun, the morning star among clouds, a dish of gold, an olive tree. . . . That, gentlemen, is how it was in the Temple, and how it will be again after the coming of Messiah. We learn it"—he tapped his book—"in *Mishna Yoma, Yoma*—Targum for Day, *yom hakipurim*, but whose is the atonement, whose is the cleansing? Does the goat for Azazel atone, does the *kohen gadol* cleanse and hallow us? No, only the Most High can cleanse, only we ourselves can atone. Rabbi Akiva reminds us: 'Who is it that makes you clean? Our Father in Heaven.' So why, gentlemen, do you suppose the Temple was even then necessary, why the goats, the bullock, the blood? Why is it necessary for all of this to be restored by Messiah? These are questions we must torment ourselves with. Which of us would slaughter an animal, not for sustenance, but for an idea? Which of us would dash an animal to its death? Which of us would not feel himself to be a sinner in doing so? Or feel the shame of Esau? You may say that those were other days, the rituals are obsolete, we are purer now, better, we do not sprinkle blood so readily. But in truth you would not say so, you would not lie. For animals we in our day substitute men.

What the word Azazel means exactly is not known—we call it wilderness, some say it is hell itself, demons live there. But whatever we mean by 'wilderness,' whatever we mean by 'hell,' surely the plainest meaning is *instead of*. Wilderness instead of easeful places, hell and devils instead of plenitude, life, peace. Goat instead of man. Was there no one present in the Temple who, seeing the animals in all their majesty of health, shining hair, glinting hooves, timid nostrils, muscled like ourselves, gifted with tender eyes no different from our own, the whole fine creature trembling— was there no one there when the knife slit the fur and skin and the blood fled upward who did not feel the splendor of the living beast? Who was not in awe of the miracle of life turned to carcass? Who did not think: *how like that goat I am! The goat goes, I stay, the goat instead of me.* Who did not see in the goat led to Azazel his own destiny? Death takes us too at random, some at the altar, some over the cliff. . . . Gentlemen, we are this moment so to speak in the Temple, the Temple devoid of the Holy of Holies—when the Temple was destroyed it forsook the world, so the world itself had no recourse but to pretend to be the Temple by mockery. In the absence of Messiah there can be no *kohen gadol*, we have no authority to bless multitudes, we are not empowered, we cannot appeal except for ourselves, ourselves alone, in isolation, in futility, instead we are like the little goats, we are assigned our lot, we are designated for the altar or for Azazel, in either case we are meant to be cut down. . . . O little fathers, we cannot choose, we are driven, we are not free, we are only *instead of*: we stand *instead of*, instead of choice we have the yoke, instead of looseness we are pointed the way to go, instead of freedom we have the red cord around our throats, we were in villages, they drove us into camps, we were in trains, they drove us into showers of poison, in the absence of Messiah the secular ones made a nation, enemies bite at it. All that we do without Messiah is in vain. When the Temple forsook the world, and the world presumed to mock the Temple, everyone on earth became a goat or a bullock, he-animal or she-animal, all our prayers are bleats and neighs on the way to a forsaken altar, a teeming Azazel. Little fathers! How is it possible to live? When will Messiah come? You! You! Visitor! You're looking somewhere else, who are you not to look?"

He was addressing Bleilip—he pointed a finger without a nail.

"Who are you? Talk and look! Who!"

Bleilip spoke his own name and shook: a schoolboy in a schoolroom. "I'm here with the deepest respect, Rabbi. I came out of interest for your community."

"We are not South Sea islanders, sir, our practices are well known since Sinai. You don't have to turn your glance. We are not something new in the world."

"Excuse me, Rabbi, not new—unfamiliar."

"To you."

"To me," Bleilip admitted.

"Exactly my question! Who are you, what do you represent, what are you to us?"

"A Jew. Like yourselves. One of you."

"Presumption! Atheist, devourer! For us there is the Most High, joy, life. For us trust! But you! A moment ago I spoke your own heart for you, *emes?*"

Bleilip knew this word: truth, true, but he was only a visitor and did not want so much: he wanted only what he needed, a certain piece of truth, not too big to swallow. He was afraid of choking on more. The rebbe said, "You believe the world is in vain, *emes?*"

"I don't follow any of that, I'm not looking for theology—"

"Little fathers," said the rebbe, "everything you heard

me say, everything you heard me say in a voice of despair,
emanates from the liver of this man. My mouth made itself
his parrot. My teeth became his beak. He fills the study-
house with a black light, as if he keeps a lump of radium
inside his belly. He would eat us up. Man he equates with
the goats. The Temple, in memory and anticipation, he considers an abattoir. The world he regards as a graveyard. You
are shocked, Mister Bleilip, that I know your kidneys, your
heart? Canker! Onset of cholera! You say you don't come for
'theology,' Mister Bleilip, and yet you have a particular conception of us, *emes?* A certain idea."

Bleilip wished himself mute. He looked at Yussel, but
Yussel had his eyes on his sleeve-button.

"Speak in your own language, please"—Bleilip was unable to do anything else—"and I will understand you very
well. Your idea about us, please. Stand up!"

Bleilip obeyed. That he obeyed bewildered him. The cres-
cents of faces in profile on either side of him seemed sharp as
scythes. His yarmulka fell off his head but, rising, he failed
to notice it—one of the men quickly clapped it back on. The
stranger's palm came like a blow.

"Your idea," the rebbe insisted.

"Things I've heard," Bleilip croaked. "That in the Zohar
it's written how Moses coupled with the Shekhina on Mount
Sinai. That there are books to cast lots by, to tell fortunes,
futures. That some Rabbis achieved levitation, hung in air
without end, made babies come in barren women, healed
miraculously. That there was once a Rabbi who snuffed out
the Sabbath light. Things," Bleilip said, "I suppose legends."

"Did you hope to witness any of these things?"

Bleilip was silent.

"Then let me again ask. Do you credit any of these
things?"

"Do you?" asked Bleilip.

Yussel intervened: "Forbidden to mock the rebbe!"

But the rebbe replied, "I do not believe in magic. That there are influences I do believe."

Bleilip felt braver. "Influences?"

"Turnings. That a man can be turned from folly, error, wrong choices. From misery, evil, private rage. From a mistaken life."

Now Bleilip viewed the rebbe; he was suspicious of such hands. The hands a horror: deformity, mutilation: caught in what machine?—and above them the worker's cap. But otherwise the man seemed simple, reasoned, balanced, after certain harmonies, sanities, the ordinary article, no mystic, a bit bossy, pedagogue, noisy preacher. Bleilip, himself a man with a profession and no schoolboy after all, again took heart. A commonplace figure. People did what he asked, nothing more complicated than this—but he had to ask. Or tell, or direct. A monarch perhaps. A community needs to be governed. A human relationship: of all words Bleilip, whose vocabulary was habitually sociological, best of all liked "relationship."

He said, "I don't have a mistaken life."

"Empty your pockets."

Bleilip stood without moving.

"Empty your pockets!"

"Rabbi, I'm not an exercise, I'm not a demonstration—"

"Despair must be earned."

"I'm not in despair," Bleilip objected.

"To be an atheist is to be in despair."

"I'm not an atheist, I'm a secularist," but even Bleilip did not know what he meant by this.

"Esau! For the third time: empty your pockets!"

Bleilip pulled the black plastic thing out and threw it on the table. Instantly all the men bent away from it.

"A certain rebbe," said the rebbe very quietly, "believed

every man should carry two slips of paper in his pockets. In one pocket should be written: 'I am but dust and ashes.' In the other: 'For my sake was the world created.' This canker fills only one pocket, and with ashes." He picked up Bleilip's five-and-ten gun and said "Esau! Beast! Lion! To whom did you intend to do harm?"

"Nobody," said Bleilip out of his shame. "It isn't real. I keep it to get used to. The feel of the thing. Listen," he said, "do you think it's easy for me to carry that thing around and keep on thinking about it?"

The rebbe tried the trigger. It gave out a tin click. Then he wrapped it in his handkerchief and put it in his pocket. "We will now proceed with *ma'ariv*," he said. "The study hour is finished. Let us not learn more of this matter. This is Jacob's tent."

The men left the study table and took up their old places, reciting. Bleilip, humiliated (the analogy to a teacher confiscating a forbidden toy was too exact), still excited, the tremor in his groin worse, was in awe before this incident. Was it amazing chance that the rebbe had challenged the contents of his pockets, or was he a seer? At the conclusion of *ma'ariv* the men dispersed quickly; Bleilip recognized from Yussel's white stare that this was not the usual way. He felt like an animal they were running from. He intended to run himself—all the way to the Greyhound station—but the rebbe came to him. "You," he said (*du*, as if to an animal, or to a child, or to God), "the other pocket. The second one. The other side of your coat."

"What?"

"Disgorge."

So Bleilip took it out. And just as the toy gun could instantly be seen to be a toy, all tin glint, so could this one be seen for what it was: monstrous, clumsy and hard, heavy, with a scarred trigger and a barrel that smelled. Dark, no gleam. An actuality, a thing for use. Yussel moaned, dipping his head up and down. "In my house! Stood in front of my wife with it! With two!"

"With one," said the rebbe. "One is a toy and one not, so only one need be feared. It is the toy we have to fear: the incapable—"

Yussel broke in, "We should call the police, rebbe."

"Because of a toy? How they will laugh."

"But the other! This!"

"Is it capable?" the rebbe asked Bleilip.

"Loaded, you mean? Sure it's loaded."

"Loaded, you hear him?" Yussel said. "He came as a curiosity-seeker, rebbe, my wife's cousin, I had no suspicion of this—"

The rebbe said, "Go home, Yussel. Go home, little father."

"Rebbe, he can shoot—"

"How can he shoot? The instrument is in my hand."

It was. The rebbe held the gun—the real one. Again Bleilip was drawn to those hands. This time the rebbe saw. "Buchenwald," he said. "Blocks of ice, a freezing experiment. In my case only to the elbow, but others were immersed wholly and perished. The fingers left are toy fingers. That is why you have been afraid of them and have looked away."

He said all this very clearly, in a voice without an opinion.

"Don't talk to him, rebbe!"

"Little father, go home."

"And if he shoots?"

"He will not shoot."

Alone in the schoolhouse with the rebbe—how dim the bulbs, dangling on cords—Bleilip regretted that because of the dishonor of the guns. He was pleased that the rebbe had dismissed Yussel. The day (but now it was night) felt full of miracles and lucky chances. Thanks to Yussel he had gotten to the rebbe. He never supposed he would get to the rebbe himself—all his hope was only for a glimpse of the effect of the rebbe. Of influences. With these he was satisfied. He said again, "I don't have a mistaken life."

The rebbe enclosed the second gun in his handkerchief. "This one has a bad odor."

"Once I killed a pigeon with it."

"A live bird?"

"You believers," Bleilip threw out, "you'd cut up those goats all over again if you got the Temple back!"

"Sometimes," the rebbe said, "even the rebbe does not believe. My father when he was the rebbe also sometimes did not believe. It is characteristic of believers sometimes not to believe. And it is characteristic of unbelievers some-times to believe. Even you, Mister Bleilip—even you now and then believe in the Holy One, Blessed Be He? Even you now and then apprehend the Most High?"

"No," Bleilip said; and then: "Yes."

"Then you are as bloody as anyone," the rebbe said (it was his first real opinion), and with his terrible hands put the bulging white handkerchief on the table for Bleilip to take home with him, for whatever purpose he thought he needed it.

(1970)

An Education

I · **There are at least a couple of perfect moments** in any life, and the one Una Meyer counted as second-best was a certain image of herself entering her college Latin class. It is a citified February morning. The classroom is in a great drab building, not really a skyscraper but high above the nearest church-tower, and the window looks out on the brick solemnity of an airshaft. A draft of worn cafeteria coffee slides by. Una is wearing a new long-sleeved dress with a patent-leather belt; the sleeves and the belt are somehow liberating and declare her fate to her. Besides, she is the only one in the class who can tell the difference between synecdoche and metonymy. One is the-part-for-the-whole, the other is the-sign-for-the-thing. Her body is a series of exquisitely strung bones. Her face has that double plainness of innocence and ordinariness. Her brain is deliciously loaded with Horace—wit, satire, immortality—and even more deliciously with Catullus—sparrows and lovers and a thousand kisses, and yet again a thousand, which no mean and jinxing spy shall ever see. Una has kissed no one but her parents, but she is an intellectual and the heiress of all the scholars who ever lived. The instructor's name is Mr. Collie. He is Roger Ascham resurrected. He is violent with Mr. Organski, who never prepares the lesson and can't manage case-endings. Mr. Collie is terribly strict and terribly exacting. Everything must be rendered precisely. When he turns his back, Mr. Organski spits in the air. The class shudders with indifference. "You're late," says Mr. Collie in open joy. He never tolerates lateness in anyone else, but he can't conceal his delight at seeing Una in the doorway at last. He teaches only Una. "*Tell* Mr. Organski, won't you, *why* he may not use the accusative case with the verb I've just taken the great trouble to conjugate for him on the blackboard? *Oblige* him, Miss Meyer, won't you?" Mr. Organski patiently wipes the excess spit from his mouth. He is a foreigner and a veteran; he is a year older than Mr. Collie and has a mistress, which would disgust Mr. Collie if he knew. In spite of everything Mr. Organski does not hate Una, who is now hiking up her eyeglasses by pushing on the nosepiece. He pities her because she is so skinny; she reminds him of a refugee survivor. "Well it takes the genitive," Una says, and thinks: If only the universe would stay as it is this moment! Only a tiny handful of very obscure verbs—who can remember them?—take the genitive. Una is of the elect who can remember. And she is dazzled—how poignantly she senses her stupendous and glorious fate! How tenderly she contemplates her mind!

That is the sort of girl Una Meyer was at eighteen.

At twenty-four she hadn't improved. By then she had a master's degree in Classics and most of a Ph.D.—the only thing left was to write the damn dissertation. Her subject was certain Etruscan findings in southern Turkey. Their remarkable interest lay in the oddity that all the goddesses seemed to be left-handed. Una, who was right-handed, felt she must be present at the dig—she was waiting for her Fulbright to come through. No one doubted it would, but all the same Una was positive she had deteriorated. It was summer. Her dissertation adviser and his wife Betty and sons Bruce and Brian had rented a cottage on Martha's Vineyard. The younger teachers had taken a house on Fire Island; no one had invited Una. The department office was empty most of the day, and a pneumatic drill in the street below roared and rattled the paper clips in the desk-drawers, so Una took to spending her afternoons in the college cafeteria. In six years the coffee had aged a bit—you could tell by the brittle staleness meandering through the cigarette smells—but never Una. She still thought of herself as likely to be damaged by caffeine, and she said she hated lipstick because it was savagery to paint oneself brighter than one was born, but mainly she was against coal tar.

And that was how she came to notice Rosalie. Rosalie was one of those serious blue-eyed fat girls, very short-fingered, who seem to have arrived out of their mothers' wombs with ten years' experience at social work. She wore her hair wrapped in a skimpy braid around her big head, which counted against her, but she was reading *Coming of Age in Samoa* in paperback, a good point in a place where all the other girls were either paring or comparing—nails or engagement rings as the case might be. It wasn't the engaged girls that made Una feel she had declined—what she felt for *them* was scorn. She was sure they would all marry nightgown salesmen or accountants from the School of Business Administration; not one of them would ever get to Turkey to study left-handed Etruscan goddesses. But all the same she was depressed. Her life struck her as very ordinary —nowadays practically everyone she was acquainted with could tell the difference between synecdoche and metonymy (that was what came of being a graduate student), but the sad thing was it no longer seemed important. That was her trouble: the importance of everything had fallen. And worse than that, she had a frightening secret—she was afraid she really didn't care enough about her dissertation subject. And she was afraid she would get dysentery in Turkey, even though she had already promised her mother to boil everything. She almost wished she was stupid and fit only to be engaged, so that she wouldn't have to win a Fulbright.

Rosalie, meanwhile, had come to page 95, and was gulping a lemonade without looking; when the straw gargled loudly she knew she had attained the end of her nourishment, and let go. The straw, though bitten, was a clean yellow. Una, whom the sight of lipstick on straws offended, decided Rosalie might be interesting to talk to.

"You realize Margaret Mead's a waste of time," she began. "There aren't any *standards* in cultural anthropology" —this was just to start the argument off—"that's what's wrong with it."

Rosalie showed no surprise at being addressed that way, out of the blue. "That's the idea," she said. "That's the way it's supposed to be. Cultural relativity. Whatever is, is. What's wrong in New York can be right in Zanzibar."

"I don't go for that," Una said. "That sounds pretty depraved. Take murder. Murder's wrong in any culture. I believe in the perfectibility of man."

"So do I," Rosalie said.

"Then your position isn't really logical, is it? I mean if you believe in the perfectibility of man you have to believe in that very standard of perfection all peoples aspire to."

"Nobody's perfect," Rosalie said, going sour.

"I disagree with that."

"Well, name somebody who is."

"That has nothing to do with it," Una said in her most earnest style, "just because I personally don't know anybody doesn't mean they don't exist."

"They *can't* exist."

"They might if they wanted to. They exist in theory. I'm a Platonist," Una explained.

"I'm a *bezbozhnik*," Rosalie said. "That's Russian for atheist."

Una was overwhelmed. "Do you know Russian?"

"I have this pregnant friend who was studying it last year."

"Say something else."

"*Tovarichka*, I don't know anything else, I only know the names those two call me."

"Two?" Una picked up. She was very good at picking up small points and turning them into jokes. "You have *two* pregnant friends who speak Russian?"

"One's the husband."

"Oh," Una said, because nothing bored her more than married couples. "How come you go around with people that old?"

"*She's* twenty-three and *he's* twenty-two."

Una was impressed, not to say horrified. "That's younger than *I* am. I mean that's *very* young to cage yourself up like that. I suppose they never had a chance to get any real education or anything?"

"Mary's a lawyer and Clement—well, if you're that way about Margaret Mead I won't tell you about Clement."

"Tell!" Una said.

"Clement *studied* with Margaret Mead and got his master's in anthropology at Columbia, but then he suddenly got interested in religion—mysticism, really—and now he commutes to the Union Theological Seminary. They had to move up to Connecticut so Mary can start on her J.S.D. at Yale Law School right after the baby comes. Actually"— Rosalie's stumpy forefinger scratched at *Coming of Age in Samoa*—"this is Clement's book. He lent it to me about two months ago, but I haven't seen either of them for ages—I'm going up there this weekend and I wouldn't dare turn up without it. They're *wild* on people who borrow books and don't give them back. They've got this little card catalogue they keep, just like a library, and when you return a book they ask you *questions* about it, just to make sure you didn't borrow it for nothing."

"So you're boning up!" Una concluded. She realized she was jealous. The part about the card catalogue thrilled her. "They sound marvelous. I mean they sound really wonderful and delightful."

"They're very nice," Rosalie agreed coldly.

"What's their name? In case they get famous some day." Una always took note of potential celebrity as a sort of investment, the way some people collect art. "Their last name, I mean."

"Chimes. Like what a bell does."

"Chimes. That's beautiful."

"It was legally changed from Chaims."

"But isn't that Jewish?" Una asked. "I thought you said Union Theological Sem—"

"They're emancipated. I'm bringing them a four-pound ham. You should hear Clement on 'Heidegger and the Holocaust.'"

"Heidegger and the *what?*"

"The Holy Ghost," Rosalie said. "Clement's awfully witty."

II · The really perfect moment— the one that came just when Una had decided there were no new revelations to be had in the tired old world, and the one she promised herself she would remember forever and ever —happened on the shore of the State of Connecticut at half-past four in the afternoon. Now it is the very core of August. The sky is a speckless white cheek. Yards away the water fizzes up like soda-pop against a cozy rock in the shape of a sleeping old dog. A live young dog skids maniacally between the nibble-marks the tide has bitten into the sand. The dog's owners, a couple in their fifties, are packing up to go home. They stop for one last catch of a ball—it zooms over poor Spot's jaws, but in a second Clement has dropped *King Lear* and hypnotizes the ball: it seems to wait in air for him to rise and pluck it from the lip of the sun. "Good *boy*," says the man, "damn good catch. Give 'er here." Back and forth goes the ball between Clement and the stranger. The stranger's wife compliments Clement: "You got a good build, sonny," she says, "only you ruin your looks with that hairy stuff. I got a picksher of my father, he wore one of them handlebars fifty years back. What's a young kid like you want with that? Take my advice, shave it off, sonny." Clement returns to the blanket grinning—how forbearing he is with his inferiors! How graceful! He is a thick-thighed middle-sized young man who looks like the early Mark Twain; he is even beginning crinkles around his eyes, and he is egalitarian with kings and serfs. Una has been in Connecticut only an hour, but he is as comradely toward her as though they had been friends since spherical trigonometry. Mary is a bit cooler. There has been the smallest misunderstanding: the Chimeses were honestly under the impression that Rosalie said on the phone she was bringing a Turk. Mary expected a woman in purdah, and here is only bony Una in a bathing suit. The Chimeses have had Indians, Chinese, Malayans, Chileans, Arabs (especially these: on the Israeli question they are pro-Arab); they have not yet had any Turks. Una is a disappointment, but since she doesn't know it, she continues in her rapture without a fault. They go back to reading the play aloud. There are only three copies; Mary and Una share one. Una scarcely dares to peek at Mary, her voice is so dramatic, but she sees a little of her teeth, which are very large and unabashed, perfect teeth unlike anyone else's; cav-

ities in Mary's teeth are inconceivable. The baby she is har-
boring under her smock is also very large and unabashed,
and Mary, to accommodate its arc, leans down hard on one
elbow, like a mermaid. Mary is beautiful. Her nose is ideally
made and her eyes have broad skeptical lids that close as
slowly as garret shutters. Amazingly, a child's laugh leaps
from her mouth. Una is embarrassed when her own turn
comes, but then she is relieved—Rosalie doesn't act well at
all. Rosalie plays Goneril, Una is Regan, Clement is Cor-
delia, Mary is King Lear. "I prithee, daughter, do not make
me mad," Mary says to Rosalie, "thou art a boil, a plague-
sore, an embossed carbuncle," and they all four screech with
hilarity. Mary's giggle runs higher and lasts longer than anyone's. "Mary went to a special drama school when she was
ten," Clement explains. "Clement sings," Mary informs Una.
"We ought to do a play with songs. He's got this marvelous
baritone but you have to beg him." "Next time we'll do the
Beggar's Opera," Clement teases. A little wind comes flying
over them, raising a veil of sand. "Time to go home, you'll be
cold, bunny," Clement tells Mary. He stretches across fat
Rosalie to kiss the pink heel of Mary's foot, and in the very
next moment, when they all slap their Shakespeares down
and tussle with the pockets in the sand as they scramble up,
a brilliance is revealed to Una. All the world's gold occupies
the sky. The cooling sun drops a notch lower. They head for
the iron staircase that leads to the Chimeses' seaside apartment, and Una carries in her ribs a swelling secret. Her
whole long-ago sense of illimitable possibility is restored to
her. It is as though she has just swallowed Beauty. A charm
of ecstasy has her in thrall. She has fallen in love with the
Chimeses, the two of them together. Oh, the two of them
together!

They were perfect. Everything about them was perfect.
Una had never before seen so enchanting an apartment: it

was exactly right, just what you would expect of a pair of intellectual lovers. Instead of pictures on the walls, there were two brightly crude huge rectangles of tapestry, with abstract designs in them. Clement had sewn them. On the inside of the bathroom door, where vain people stupidly hang mirrors, Mary had painted a Mexican-style mural, with overtones of Dali. And all along the walls, in the kitchen and the bedroom and the living room and even in the little connecting corridor, were rows and rows of bookshelves nailed together very serviceably by Clement. Clement could build a bookcase, Mary said, in two hours flat. Meanwhile Rosalie was in the kitchen checking on the ham, which they had left cooking all afternoon.

"Is it done?" Mary asked from the bathroom.

"I'd guess another fifteen minutes," Rosalie said.

"Then I'm going to shower. You're next, Rosalie. Then Una. Then Clement."

Una went prowling among the books. Regiments of treasure marched by. The Chimeses had the entire original New York edition of Henry James. They had Jones's life of Freud. They had Christmas Humphreys on Buddhism, *Memoirs of Hecate County*, four feet of Balzac, a volume of Sappho translated into Mandarin on the facing pages, and a whole windowsill's length of advanced mathematics. There were several histories of England and plenty of Fichte and Schelling. There was half a wall of French.

Between a copy of *Das Kapital* and a pale handbook called "How to Become an Expert Electrician for Your Own Home Purposes in Just Thirty Minutes," Una discovered the card catalogue Rosalie had told her about. It was in a narrow green file box from Woolworth's. "What a fabulous idea," Una said, flipping through the cards. She adored anything alphabetical.

"We've only just started on our record collection. We've

got about a thousand records and we're going to catalogue the whole shebang," Clement said.

The bathroom door clattered. "Your turn!" Mary yelled —Una had never known anyone to bathe so quickly. Out came Mary wrapped in a Chinese bathrobe, with her long dark hair pinned up. She smelled like a piney woods.

Rosalie said she didn't see the necessity of showering, she hadn't been on the beach an hour.

"You haven't improved a bit," Mary complained. "We *always* used to have to coax Rosalie to take baths."

"In our other apartment," Clement said.

"*My* apartment," Rosalie growled from under the shower. Like Mary, she kept the door open.

"Rosalie was paying a lot less rent than we were, so we moved in with her," Mary said. "Up to two months ago we were all living together."

"Rosalie's a pretty good cook," Clement said, "but *we* taught her how to do a salad. She used to cut things up piecemeal. First the lettuce, then the cucumbers—"

"Cucumber rinds have no nutritional value whats*oever*," Mary announced, "but we keep them on for cosmetic purposes. Poor Rosalie, after we came up here she was left all alone with her chunks of piecemeal lettuce."

"Her clumsy tomato-halves," Clement said, "her big pitted black ripe olives."

"Poor Rosalie," Rosalie called. "She was left all alone with the hole in the closet door."

"We put the loudspeaker for our hi-fi in it," Clement told Una.

"They always cut holes in closet doors," Rosalie called.

Una, who was very law-abiding, was privately awed at such a glamorous affront to landlords' rights. But when Rosalie came out of the shower Una hurried in after her, so that the Chimeses wouldn't think she was one of those girls who had to be coaxed to bathe.

After supper Clement asked Una what she would like to hear, and Una, a musical nitwit, timidly said *The Mikado*. "Is that all right for you?" she wondered.

"Oh, we like everything," Clement said. "Bach, jazz, blues—"

"What you want to remember about the Chimeses," Rosalie instructed, "is that they're Renaissance men, they're nothing if not well-rounded."

"Especially me," said Mary. She tossed out one of her childlike giggles and suddenly sat down on the floor in frog-position and puffed very fast, like a locomotive, while Clement counted up to fifty. "That's for painless childbirth. You anticipate the contractions," he said, and put on *The Mikado*. Mary's legs rolled in the air. "Listen, bunny, Una said she's going to help organize the record catalogue."

Una flushed. She didn't remember saying it, but she *had* thought it—it was exactly what she hoped they would ask her to do. It was wonderful that Clement had guessed.

"Not me," said Rosalie, and spread herself on the sofa. Una decided Rosalie was terrifically lazy and not very sociable, and to show the Chimeses *she* wasn't at all like that, she squatted right down on the floor next to Mary and prepared for business. Mary gave Una a pile of index cards and her own fountain pen, and Clement took the records out of their folders and read out the date of issuance, the Köchel number, and all sorts of complicated-sounding musical information Una had never before encountered.

"We're going to index by cross-reference," Mary said. "Composer's name by alphabet, name of piece by order of composition, and then a list of our personal record-numbers by order of date of purchase. That way we'll know whether

they're scratchy because of being worn or because of difficulties in the system itself."

Una hardly understood a word, but she went on gamely
making notes, until Clement finally discovered she was no
good for anything but alphabetizing.

"You could use her for your bibliographical index, she'd
be fine for that," Mary suggested. "Do you know John Liv-
ingston Lowes's *The Road to Xanadu?* Well, Clement's
doing something like that. He's working on the sources of
Paul Tillich's thought."

Una said that must be pretty interesting, but unless you
were a mind-reader how could you find them out?

"I'm researching all the books he's ever read. It's a very
intricate problem. I'm in constant correspondence with him."

"You mean he sends you *letters?*" Una cried. "Paul *Tillich*, the philosopher?"

"No, he communicates by carrier-pigeon. And it's Paul
Tillich the president of the carpenters' union," Clement said.
"My God, girl, you need educating."

"Especially in library science," Rosalie sneered from the
sofa.

But Una was stirred. "That's really *doing* something. It's
thinking about the world. I mean it's really scholarship!"

"Don't you like what you're doing?" Clement asked.

"I don't. Oh, I don't. I'm sick to death of Latin and Greek
and I don't give a damn about the Etruscan Aphrodite and
I'm scared silly about getting a Turkish disease," she burst
out. "Oh, I envy you two, I really do. You have a passion and
you go right ahead with it, you're doing exactly what you
want to do, you're right in the middle of being alive."

Mary said gravely, "You should never do what you don't
want to do. You should never go against your own nature."

"It's the same as going against God," Clement said.

Rosalie tumbled off the sofa. "Oh God. If we're on God again I'm going home."

"I feel," Clement said, "that the teleological impulse in the universe definitely includes man."

Rosalie turned up the Lord High Executioner's volume.

"The thing is," Mary said, "if you're going after your Ph.D. only for fashionable reasons or prestige reasons you should give it up."

"I've got these fabulous recommendations," Una said morosely. "I'm probably going to *get* the damn Fulbright."

"You should give it up," Mary insisted.

Una had never considered this. It was logical, but it didn't occur to her that anyone ever took logic seriously enough to live by it. "I'd have to do something else instead. I don't know what I'd do," she argued.

"Find somebody and get married." This was Rosalie, that traitor. She was no different from all those other girls who came down to the cafeteria to show off their new rings. Probably she wished she had one herself, but she was too fat, and no one would so much as blink at her. The only reason Rosalie didn't wear lipstick was that Mary didn't. The only reason Una had been attracted to Rosalie in the first place was that Rosalie had been reading Clement's book. What a fake! What a hypocrite! Rosalie was a toad in Chimeses' clothing. Una felt the strictest contempt for herself—she had let that sly girl take her in. She was astonished that the Chimeses could ever have endured living with Rosalie, she was so ordinary. She wondered that they hadn't dropped her long ago. It only proved how incredibly superior they were. They always looked for the right motives not to do a thing.

"Marriage is exactly *not* the point," Clement snapped. Una could see he was just as impatient with Rosalie as she was, but he smothered his disgust in philosophy. "It's not a question of externals, it's a question of internals. Going to Turkey is an external solution. Getting married is an external solution. But the problem *of* the Self requires a solution *for* the Self, you can see that, can't you?"

Una wasn't sure. "But I wouldn't know what to *do*," she wailed.

"In an existential dilemma it isn't action that's called for, it's *in*action. Nonaction. Stasis. Don't think about what you ought to do, think about what you ought *not* to do. —Come on, Rosalie, cut out the noise, lower that damn thing down. What I mean," Clement said, "is stop looking at the world in terms of your own self-gratification. It's God's world, not yours."

"God knows it's not mine," Rosalie said. She reduced Nanki-Poo's song to the size of an ant's—she seemed good-natured enough, but really she had no mind of her own: she did whatever anyone told her to do. "If I owned the world Clement would've cut a hole in it by now."

Una was shocked. Here was a fresh view! And it was true, it was true, she was too proud, she had always thought of her own gratification. Clement was so clever he could look right through her. But all the same she was a little flattered —she had never before been in an existential dilemma. "I've always been very careerist," she admitted. "I guess the thing I've cared about most is getting some sort of recognition."

"You won't get it in Turkey," Mary warned, but her voice was now very kind.

"You'll get buried same as those left-handed Etruscans," Clement said.

This made Una laugh. Oh, they were perfect!

"Take my advice," Rosalie said. "Get your degree and be a teacher."

"Rosalie means be like Rosalie," Clement said.

"There's worse," Rosalie said.

"I'll give it up," Una said, but the momentousness of this was somehow lost, because Mary suddenly clapped the knot of her piled-up hair and shrieked "Breakfast! Clement, what'll we do for breakfast? There's not a scrap."

"I'll bicycle out to the market in the morning."

"Oh, I'll go," Una offered, charmed at the picture of herself pedaling groceries in the basket before her. It would almost make her one of them. "I'm a very early riser."

"There's not a scrap of cash either," Mary said ruefully. "Clement's scholarship money comes quarterly, and my scholarship money comes every month, but it doesn't start till the term starts. We were *counting* on Rosalie's bringing the ham, but I spent the last penny on tonight's baked beans."

"It wasn't your fault, bunny. And it wasn't the beans that did it, it was the wine I bought day before yesterday. Hell with budgets anyhow—come on, let's have the wine!"

"Here's to Una Meyer," Clement sing-songed, and Una glowed, because it was plain her cataclysmic avowal hadn't been overlooked after all. "Drink to Una on the Brink."

"Of disaster," Rosalie purred.

"Of Selfhood," Clement declared, and Una was nearly embarrassed with the pleasure of her importance. The wine was a rosé and seemed to blush for her. Mary poured it out in pretty little goblets, which she explained were the product of a brand-new African glass industry, and not only helped to make a budding economy viable, but were much cheaper than they looked. All at once the four of them were having a party. They switched off the record-player, and Clement, after only two or three pleas from Mary, sang a comic version of an old-time movie version of "The Road to

Mandalay." He sounded exactly like a witty Nelson Eddy. Then he took down his guitar from its special hook next to the towel-rack in the bathroom and they all joined in on "On Top of Old Smoky," "Once I Wore My Apron Low," "Jimmy Crack Corn," "When I Was a Bachelor," and a lot of others, and by the time Clement carried in the folding cot for Una and Mary covered the sofa pillow with a clean pillowcase for Rosalie, Una was happier than she had ever been in her life, until a wonderful thing happened. It touched her so much she almost wept with sentiment. When all the lights were off and everyone was very still, Clement and Mary came softly out of their bedroom in their pajamas, and, one by one, they kissed Una and Rosalie as though they had been their own dear children.

"Goodnight," Mary whispered.

"Goodnight," Una whispered back.

"Goodnight," Clement said.

"Goodnight," Rosalie said, but even in the dark, without seeing the sarcastic bulge of her neck, Una thought Rosalie sounded stubbornly unmoved.

"Rosalie honey," Clement said tenderly, "can you lend us five for breakfast?"

"All I've got's my trainfare back," Rosalie said in the most complacent tone imaginable. Una was certain Rosalie was lying for her own malicious ends, whatever they could be.

"Oh, let *me*, please," she cried, sitting upright very fast. "Listen, Clement, where do you keep your bikes? I'll get everything the minute I'm up."

"We wouldn't think of it," Mary said in her steadfast way. "It isn't just breakfast, you know, it's practically the whole week till Clement's check comes."

No one was whispering now.

"Oh, *please*," Una said. "I'd really like to, honest. I mean before today you didn't know me from a hole in the wall—"

"In the door," Rosalie crowed.

"—and you gave me all this marvelous hospitality and everything. It's only right."

"Well," Clement said—he seemed very stern, almost like a father—"if you really want to. Only don't forget the eggs."

"Oh, I won't," Una promised, and could hardly fall asleep waiting for the next day of living in the Chimeses' aura to begin.

III · **Early in the fall** the Chimeses moved into New Haven proper, which was a relief for everyone, but for no one more than Una, who hadn't really minded nights on the sofa until they had had to put the crib right up against her feet. There was no other place for it. The Chimeses' seaside bedroom, though it had a romantic view of the waves, was only a cubicle with a window —there wasn't even a cranny with a dresser in it, much less a crib. In New Haven they found a downtown tenement that was cheap and by comparison almost spacious. In the new flat there were three bedrooms: one for the Chimeses', one was a study for Mary, and the one farthest from this, to keep the noise at a distance, was the baby's. Clement bought a second-hand screen and put it between Una's bed and the crib— "to give the infant its privacy," he joked.

The birth itself had been remarkable—all the nurses agreed the hospital had never had anyone to match Mary. She was over and done with it in an hour, and with hardly any fuss. Mary attributed this to having learned how to deal with the contractions, and Clement, who had turned more ebullient than ever, laughed and said Mary had practiced with can't, won't, and ain't.

The baby, of course, was magnificent. It was unusually beautiful for a small infant and had long limbs. Mary had all along been indifferent to its sex, but Clement claimed he needed to free himself of potential incest-fantasies by releasing them into reality: he had wanted a girl from the start. Mary, Una, and Clement argued about names for days, and finally compromised on Christina, after the heroine of *The Princess Casamassima*. Christina, as a combination of two perfections, was exactly what Una had expected, and she looked at her as on some sacred object which she was not allowed to touch too often. But soon Mary decided that she had to spend more and more time in the law library, so she let Una wheel Christina around and around the streets near the university for a couple of hours every day.

Una had the time for it now: Clement had made up his mind not to finish his bibliographical index. His correspondence had waned, and to Una's surprise it turned out that the letters weren't really from Tillich, but from his secretary. Clement said this was just like all theologians: their whole approach was evasive, you could see it right in their titles. *The Courage to Be*, Clement said, was a very ambiguous book, and if the *product* was that ambiguous, you could hardly follow up the sources, could you? He told Una he would have dropped the project as futile long ago if she hadn't taken such an interest in the way he went about it. In the beginning he spent hours typing involved letters on this or that point to obscure academics with names like Knoll or Creed, but after a while he discovered he could think better if he dictated and Una typed. Anyhow he was always having to run off and help Mary with the baby, or else he had to stop in the middle of a sentence to carry a big bundle of diapers to the laundromat. Gradually Una could complete his abandoned phrases without him. She got so good at this that the two of them had a little conspiracy: Una worked out the letters in Clement's style, all on her own, and Clement signed them. He often praised her, and said she could follow up leads even better than he could. Now and then he told her she wrote very well for a nonwriter, and at those moments Una felt that maybe she wasn't an imposition on the Chimeses after all.

She worried about this a lot, even though they let her pay a good chunk of the rent—she had begged them so poignantly they couldn't refuse her. At first she had tried not to get in their way, and reminded them several times a day that if they regretted their invitation they shouldn't hesitate a wink in withdrawing it. She still couldn't believe that they actually *wanted* her to live with them. They were always comparing her to Rosalie and reminding themselves what a nasty temper Rosalie sometimes had. Rosalie used to like to sleep to the last minute, when she realized perfectly well that they *depended* on her for breakfast—at that time they'd both had very tough schedules, much tougher than that sluggard Rosalie's, and if they missed breakfast they wouldn't eat again until supper. They had a lot of other Rosalie stories, all terrible. Una determined to be as unlike Rosalie as possible—for instance, she took to preparing breakfast every day, even though Mary and Clement were both shocked at her zeal and told her it wasn't in the least bit necessary. But Mary observed that if Una was going to be up anyway, she might as well give Christina her seven o'clock bottle, which would mean Una's getting up only fifteen minutes earlier than she had to to make the breakfast. Sometimes it was three-quarters-of-an-hour earlier, but Una didn't mind—whenever she lifted Christina she felt she was holding treasure. She knew Christina would turn out to be extraordinary.

Besides, she wanted to be as useful as possible, considering how Clement was sweating to get her some sort of subfellowship from the seminary. It was only fair, he said, now that she was doing practically half his work, even though it was the superficial half. He took the train to New York three days a week, and every time he returned it was with a solemn anger. "They're trying to get me to believe their budget's closed," he would say. Or, "Damn them, they don't realize the caliber of what I'm *doing*. They say they don't give money for research assistants to anyone lower than associate professor. That's a lot of baloney. Don't worry about it, Una, we'll get something for you." Una said it was all right—so far she still had some money in the bank account her grandmother had started for her: every year on Una's birthday or on holidays her grandmother had put in seventy-five dollars. Mary said it was a shame Una's grandmother was dead. "People don't *need* grandmothers any more," Clement said, "they've got fellowships nowadays." "If Una were getting her Fulbright money right now, it would help," Mary said in a voice a little more pinched than her usual one. "If Una were getting her Fulbright money right now," Clement noted, "she'd be in Turkey, and where would *we* be? —Look, I'll beat them down somehow, don't you worry about the moolah, Una."

Whenever the Chimeses mentioned her lost Fulbright— it *seemed* often, but it wasn't really—Una felt guilty. Just as she feared, she had won the thing, and her adviser came back from Martha's Vineyard with his wife and boys and flew into a fury. He called Una a fool and a shirker for saying she'd pass up a prize like that, and for what? It was only an honor and not life, Una said. He asked whether the real point wasn't that she was going off to be married like all of them. He said he was against women in universities anyhow; they couldn't be trusted to get on with their proper affairs. Her real trouble, he told her, was she didn't have the guts to settle down to hard work. Sometimes Una wondered whether any of this was true. She was busy with domestic details—washing up, making the beds, tending the baby (of course it wasn't *just* a baby), exactly like a married person. And even though helping Clement on top of all the rest wore her out, still that sort of thing didn't count as *work*, since she didn't really understand what it was he was getting at. Clement had explained that he couldn't take the time to show her the basic insight of his project, it was too complex for a philosophical novice, and without it she couldn't hope to get near the nerve of his idea. That was why, he reminded her, she mustn't expect more than a pittance of the sum he was demanding for her from the seminary.

But one day Clement stomped off the train and said he was never going back. They had suspended him.

"But why?" Una exclaimed. The first thought she had was that Clement had finally gone too far on her behalf. "Is it on account of badgering them all the time? The money I mean," she said in her shame.

"Don't be silly, it has nothing to do with you, why should it?"

"Haven't you noticed, Una?" Mary said. She wasn't a bit upset. "Clement's been losing his faith. He's been intellectualizing about it too much—that's always the first sign."

"I finally had to speak up in Systematic Dogmatics," Clement said modestly. "I told old Hodges today I didn't think he or any of them actually knew what the Gnostics were *after*. Well, he let on about it to the Dean, and the Dean called me in and asked whether I was really on the road to Damascus. 'The fact is,' I said, 'I don't feel the present ministry's coming to grips with the problem of the *Trinity*, sir.' And you know what the old baboon answers? 'Suppose we respect those feelings for a year or two, Mr. Chimes. If you're not at home with the Gnostics by then maybe you'd be better off among the *a*gnostics.' Very funny. I resigned then and there."

"And about time," Mary said.

"How humiliating!" Una cried. "How awful!" But Clement was wearing a hurt look, and immediately she understood she had made a mistake. She was sure he was offended.

"You think too much about status. Society may look up to the ministry, but what I've gotten out of all this is that I don't look up to society."

"You can't stand still in this world," Mary put in. "You have to shed your old skin every now and then."

Una was abashed. She realized that living with the Chimeses hadn't profited her an iota. She was as uneducated as ever. She still jumped to false conclusions, and she still needed instruction in life-values.

"Not that Clement wasn't *perfectly* right to leave," Una said quickly. It came out almost abject, and she could see Mary's teeth shine into forgiveness. Mary was so good! She was practically a saint. Just when you thought she was going to be terrifyingly severe, she turned around and gave you another chance to restore yourself to ordinary common sense.

"Fact is," Clement said, "I could never *be* part of the Establishment in any form. It's just something I've been avoiding coming face to face with. Actually I'm an anarchist."

"Now watch it," Mary said, giggling. "Una'll think you're secretly manufacturing bombs in the bathroom." The reason this was funny was that no place could have been less secret than the bathroom; Clement had taken off the door to make a desk for Mary's study.

"Let 'er think so, it's just what I intend to do."

"Make a *bomb?*" Una squealed, though she didn't feel like it. Sometimes she acted straight man just to please them.

"Exactly. A bomb called *Social Cancer.*"

"Oh, a book," Una said, since she knew Clement expected her to sound relieved. All the same she was really impressed.

"I intend to pillory the whole society from top to bottom in blank verse. It'll be an exposé of the rich and the poor, the common man and the intelligentsia—and a work of art besides. There hasn't been anything like it since Alexander Pope wrote *The Dunciad,*" Clement pointed out, "and Pope wasn't that comprehensive in his conception."

That night they celebrated Clement's new book, which he was going to start writing early the next morning. They wheeled Christina to the park and right in front of her carriage built a fire out of Clement's bibliographical index. Clement and Mary threw notebook after notebook into the fire, and Una was sad, because there were so many months of toil in them. She saw her own handwriting curl up and char—all the notes she had taken for Clement on Buber and Niebuhr and Bultmann and Karl Jaspers and Kierkegaard. She had read all those difficult philosophers for nothing.

"It's not as though you haven't been through this sort of thing yourself—you're always forgetting that," Mary said. Mary was uncanny. She always knew when Una's thoughts were limping off in the wrong direction. "You have to learn how to dispense with the past, even if outsiders say it shows personal instability. Remember the night we all drank to you? You were great that time about letting the Fulbright go," Mary said, "you were really one of us that night." Una was stunned. Mary had never before given her such a compliment. Mary was not indiscriminate with compliments at all.

"That was different," Una objected—inside herself she was wondering whether she should dare to take Mary's praise as a sign of moral improvement, but at the same time she was afraid Mary suspected her of thinking Clement unstable. If so, it was a shameful calumny, and Mary wanted Una to know it. "I wasn't *burning* anything," Una said feebly.

"Yes you were," said witty Clement: "your ships behind you!" He had hardly ever seemed more cheerful; it had happened all at once, and it was plain even to Una that he was glad to be rid of all that long theological drudgery, which had been worthless all the time, though of course it was only Una who hadn't realized it. At lunch the next day he was delightful; he joked right through his coffee and enunciated "Excoriate the corrupt republic" at Christina in a comical falsetto until she screamed. "You're taking her out, aren't you, Una? Brat can raise the dead."

"Mary said not until three o'clock." —Mary had gone off to the library at ten that morning. She was preparing a paper on the Jurisprudence of Domestic Relations. For an epigraph it had a quotation from Rousseau urging the mothers of France to nurse their own babies, but that was the only part Una could fathom; the rest of it was a forest of alien footnotes. "Christina might be catching cold," Una said. "She sneezed a couple of times, so Mary thought she ought to stay in most of the day." Una privately believed Mary was mistaken whenever she argued there was no inborn maternal instinct—Mary herself seemed to exemplify it admirably. She always knew exactly the right thing to do about Christina.

"Oh, what's the difference," Clement said. "She needs air-ing, doesn't she? Una, I'll *tell* you what you show, what you show is the definite effects of overprotectiveness in conjunction with a mother-fixation—it's a lot healthier for Christina to get a cold than a fixation, isn't it?" He waited for Una to appreciate this sally. "Take her out now, there's a honey. Can't hear myself cerebrate with all the racket."

It was true that Christina was still screaming, but Una couldn't help thinking she had been perfectly behaved before Clement had frightened her—Christina was far too young to understand Clement's humor. She went to fetch Christina's little woolen cap and booties.

"Besides," Clement said, following Una into Christina's room, "I haven't got much time. I figure I can just about get *into* the first chapter before six."

"You haven't begun it?" Una said.

"Oh, I've *begun* it, I just haven't put it down on paper yet."

"But I thought you'd already gotten to work on it," Una said, a little discomposed. "Wouldn't you be well into it by now?" Clement had locked himself up in Mary's study all morning, and Una had taken special pains to woo Christina's silence. She had played hushing games with her for three hours, and was heavy with weariness afterward. Christina woke so early nowadays that Una never really got enough sleep.

"I didn't say I didn't get to work on it," Clement gave out in his most complicated tone, the one that only pretended to pretend annoyance, but all the while was genuinely annoyed. "I said I just hadn't committed it to paper yet. Actually, Una honey, the trouble with you is you don't understand the most fundamental thing about the Muse. As per tradition, she has to be *invoked*, you silly," but he was so fresh-faced and wide awake that Una had the strangest idea.

She hardly dared to articulate it, even to herself, but what she secretly wondered was whether Clement hadn't just gone back to sleep after breakfast. Not that she minded, of course.

"I know," she said, "Creation is a Many-Staged Process."

Clement warmed to her at once after that. She was quoting one of his own mottoes, which he had painted on the kitchen canisters. Instead of FLOUR he had put "Self-Discipline is Achievement," and instead of SUGAR (but the wet paint had dripped off the brush into the canister and they had to replace the whole five pounds), "Art is Love." The line about Creation was on the teabag can.

"But look," Una said, to make it up to Clement for seeming to criticize his working-habits (not that she meant to, but for the moment she *had* forgotten about the Muse), "you don't have to quit at six. I mean can't you work right through supper if you feel like it? Mary wouldn't mind, she'd just as soon eat in the commons anyhow. I can make you a sandwich—there's some baloney, I think—and you can have supper in the study. You don't have to *stop*."

Clement smiled at her so luminously that Una was sure she had set everything to rights again. "Well, to tell the truth, Una honey," he began, "you're still just a little bit obtuse, now aren't you? Is it your grandmother's shade that's going to pay for the baloney in my sandwich? Does it reach you what the condition of the writer is vis-à-vis a society economically structured against him?"

Christina's yells grew louder and her wriggles more unwieldy as Una tried to get the bootie on her foot. Her miniature arch was aristocratically high, but Una was too shocked by Clement's words to admire it. Still, his smile continued so brilliant that she thought the whole affair must be one of his jokes—he was right about how obtuse she was.

"Tell you what," Clement offered, "I'll put you straight on something. You want to hear the real reason I got bounced from the seminary? Lo, the greed of Una Meyer. You pushed just a little bit too far—not that I ever let on about it. But you know what they accused me of? Of trying to fatten up my scholarship *by unscrupulous methods.* I never told you that, and I wouldn't be mentioning it now if you weren't so thick—"

"Oh, Clement!" Una burst out. "I had no idea. I'm so ashamed! I was afraid it was my fault, but you said—"

"Never mind," Clement said. "Don't worry about it. I think I've got a good book in me, maybe even a great one if I can get to finish it, and by hook or crook I'm *going* to finish it. Hook: I refer to the hooks they sell at the hardware counter in Woolworth's. Crook: I refer to the management of same—they're tight-fisted enough, they pay like thieves."

"Clement, what do you *mean?*"

"It's not exactly a man's job, but for a philosopher it'll have to do. At least it's evenings—six to ten. I can write all day before I have to go, and what with Mary's law school money I guess we'll manage. Now listen, Una," he said, "I'll be candid with you. This house is a complex working hive. There isn't room for parasites. Visualize, if you will, the salt-shaker."

"Work or Die," Una said with a drying mouth. "You're going to work in the *five and ten?*"

"Spinoza was a lens-grinder. Don't be so appalled. Lincoln split logs. Clement Chimes will sell hooks, locks, bolts, and all manner of chains, some of them metaphysically displayed around his neck."

"Oh, Clement! It sounds awful! What's Mary say?"

"She says A, the work is beneath Clement, a view to which Clement heartily accedes, and B, we need the cash.

That being the hard case, will you now please remove the fire-siren from the premises so I can get *some*thing done?"

"Clement," Una said—meditatively she buttoned up Christina's sweater—"if it takes you practically the whole day to get started—"

"To invoke the Muse," Clement corrected.

"—and you only *really* begin about two or maybe three and you have to leave about five-thirty to get to the Woolworth's by six—"

"Congratulations. You're getting the point," Clement said. "Education is slowly setting in."

"—it means you'll have only about two hours or so to do any work at all."

"Insufficient and unfortunate," Clement agreed.

"But what about *Social Cancer?*"

" 'Twill suffer remissions," Clement said.

That evening, at great inconvenience to Mary, who had to rush home from the library to feed Christina and put her to bed, Una started her new job at the hardware counter in Woolworth's, and sold hooks, locks, bolts, and all manner of chains.

IV · One afternoon

Una was wheeling Christina along her usual route in the streets around Yale, when she decided to try a block she had never walked on before. It led her through the campus and past some of the old buildings. The day was cold and she pushed the carriage stolidly, without looking ahead of her, until she finally pushed it right into the briefcase of a young man hurrying across the path. The bag fell open and an assortment of medical instruments lay scattered on the ground.

"Well, look who it is," said the young man in an ugly accent. He bent to retrieve his stethoscope. "Aunt? Babysitter? Unwed mother? None of the above?"

The voice was familiar. It was Mr. Organski.

"What are you doing in New Haven?" Una yelped.

"Being diligent at my Latin, as usual."

"You were terrible in Latin, you didn't go *on* with it!"

"I couldn't help it, they name diseases in it."

"Oh, you're a doctor," Una said, laughing and picking up a pair of clamps. From inside the carriage came a small sneeze.

"If I pass. So far I'm a pompous medical student. And you? Settled in New Haven? Married, I see."

Una frowned. "This is my friends' baby."

"Aha. A spinster doing a good turn. You prefer a career?"

"Well," Una said uncomfortably.

"I understand. In that case not another word. Classified information. You're a scientist with the government? They use the labs around here, I've heard. A cyclotronist perhaps. A supersonistician. In short you're not permitted to describe your work."

"It's hardware," Una muttered.

"Just as I thought. Missiles. The classicist who thinks up the tags? Titan. Nike. Mars. Don't tell me your latest, I couldn't bear the responsibility of knowing. What's the baby's tag?"

"Christina."

"Unworthy of a warhead, better return her to the pad. Take her home anyhow. Christina has a cold."

"She has this cough. Sometimes her eyes run," Una admitted.

"Your friends are dangerous madmen, why do they let her out?"

"Well, she's awfully noisy—"

"A common disease of babyhood—*infanta clamorata*—which passes with the onset of confinement in a school building—*kindergartenia absentia*."

"—and her father's writing a book."

"Aha. A question of immortality. Christina shows symptoms of mortality, however. Look, I think I'm going your way. Where are you going?"

Mr. Organski walked her home, but Una didn't invite him in. She explained she couldn't—Clement was working.

"And the female parent?"

"Studying jurisprudence."

"A remarkable family."

"It is," Una said fervently.

"They've taken you in? How fortunate for you," said Mr. Organski.

"I know," Una said.

"Yet your good fortune increases. You were born under a lucky star. This family of geniuses has taken you in but I, Organski, a failure at conjugation, am going to take you out. To the movies Saturday night, what do you say? Say thank you."

"I can't," Una said. "Clement and Mary are going. We decided on it days ago—they're so busy they hardly ever get out, I just couldn't spoil it for them."

"Aha," said Mr. Organski. "Call me Boris. We'll arrange something else immediately."

"What about your mistress?"

"My mistress?"

"You had one."

"Didn't I just say I was a failure at conjugation? I disown and disavow all previous alliances, without promising not to look forward to others more successful. Now listen carefully.

When are Clement and Mary going to have the pleasure of meeting me?"

"Well, they're both home at night, but they're usually working—"

"This will be a medical visit. About Christina."

Una said humbly, "I'm the one who takes care of her mostly. If she's sick it's really my fault."

"Fine. Then you should be present at my lecture. Time, tomorrow night. Place, the crowded apartment of Clement and Mary and Christina and Una."

"My job is at night," Una demurred.

"Aha. Night maneuvers of the hardware. Top secret. Don't tell me anything. If the government has to hide its rocket failures under cover of darkness I don't want to share in its humiliation."

"It's *Woolworth's*," Una said in exasperation.

"Thank God, an ordinary Latinist after all. *Tedium Woolworthiae*, a harmless temporary state. I offer you a consolation. I suggest, in view of my having solemnly disowned and disavowed my previous conduct, that you undertake to shape my present conduct. Praise your stars. I'm asking you to become my current mistress."

Una giggled. It sounded just like Mary's giggle.

"I assume you lend a hand in paying your friends' rent?" Mr. Organski said. "Come and pay mine. My apartment is far less crowded."

V · The Chimeses didn't like Boris at all. In the first place, he didn't think Christina was perfect. He implied, in fact, that she was much worse than perfect. He said she was malnourished and needed liquid vitamins and her left lung wasn't clear. He said he would have to come often until he was confident she was improving. He asked to see where she slept.

"The room is too small," he insisted. "And when you put a screen around the crib like that, how do you expect the poor baby to breathe?"

"The screen is to give Una privacy," Mary said viciously.

"Take it out."

"I don't see how one thin little piece of plastic could make any difference," Clement said.

"Never mind the screen. I'm talking about the bed. Take out the bed."

"It's Una's."

"Well, all *right*," Mary said, "Una can sleep on the couch again. After all, she used to."

"Maybe you'd better ask her if she minds," Boris said.

"She won't mind."

"She never minds anything."

Boris said, "That sort of person can be an awful bore."

"As a matter of fact she is," Mary said. "She's the most obsequious person I've ever known."

Boris gave a labial croak that was meant to sound sympathetic. "Impedes intimacies, I would guess."

"You're a bit on the patronizing side, aren't you?" said Mary.

"As a matter of fact," Clement said, "she does. Always underfoot."

"She's only so-so with Christina, lets her howl."

"An impediment indeed," Boris said in his medical-student style, very grand. "I suppose she cooks?"

"If you call it that. Slices baloney. Opens cans."

"An adult should never sleep near a child," Boris said firmly. "She never gave it a thought. Is her intelligence low?

I'm thinking of the kind of job she has—small metallic objects and so forth."

"Not particularly low," Clement said. "Though I wouldn't call Una *imag*inative, bunny, would you? The thing is she won a Fulbright once."

"Incredible."

"Passed it up. It was stupid, she would've seen Turkey on it."

"Mmm," Boris said, "interesting. A neighboring land. I myself am originally from Bulgaria. Of course she's too thin. She has very small breasts."

That night, when Una returned from the hardware counter—it was a whole hour later than usual—the Chimeses waylaid her in the living room and began to speak to her very sternly.

"You're not seeing the point. Listen, Una honey," Clement said, "that man is out for no good. He came sneaking around here when he knew you were out—"

"On purpose," Mary said. "Behind your back."

"Don't confuse the issue, bunny. That's the least of it. The point is he came to try to set us against you, Una. That's the point."

"It was plain as day that's what he was out for," Mary told Una. "I can't think what his motives could be."

"No motive," Clement said. "The world is full of jealous people like that. They can't bear seeing close relationships, they just have to wreck them."

"He's even trying to turn Christina against you," Mary said. "A *baby*, imagine. He thinks you contaminate her. He says you have to sleep somewhere else, for health reasons."

"There wasn't an item he didn't criticize. He just wouldn't be satisfied until he got us to say nasty things about you. Not that he managed it."

"It's written all over his face what he is," Mary said.

"He even insulted your *looks*," Clement said. "He's one of these belittlers, I know that kind. Medical types tend to think they're little gods. He said you didn't have the sense to deal with sickness. As if anybody's sick."

"If he keeps it up he'll frighten you off, Una, you'll be scared to go *near* Christina."

"He's pretty damn self-important, that guy. He's just looking to assert some so-called authority."

"Keep away from him," Mary advised.

Una thought it was odd that they were talking about Boris, whom they had only just met, exactly the way they always talked about Rosalie. "But I left him only ten minutes ago."

"Boris?" the Chimeses chimed together.

"When I came out of the Woolworth's there he was at the door."

"Waiting for you? He must've gone over right from here."

"He never said a word. Sly," Mary observed.

"We went to this place," Una explained, "for coffee. *He* had coffee," she amended; "I had cocoa."

"You see? You see?" Mary said.

"She doesn't see," Clement said. "Una honey, *look* at it, it's right under your nose. He's trying to wreck things. Like Rosalie. Didn't Rosalie tell you not to move in with us? Didn't she? You can't deny it, we *knew* it, it would be just like her. You've never been sorry you came in halfies with us, have you?"

"Gosh no," Una said gratefully, but the truth was she felt a little muddled. It was after midnight; she had sold four Phillips screwdrivers, three combination locks and an ordinary padlock, two cans of furniture polish, a wad of picture-wire, a tube of automobile touch-up, a bicycle chain, a pair of bicycle clips, a dozen boxes of thumbtacks, and one door-knob. She longed for bed.

"Stop," Mary said. "Not in there. You're not supposed to use up any more of Christina's oxygen."

"Oh," said Una, and sank down on the sofa. *Pang*, went the bad spring. Mary, whose figure was every bit as good now as before her pregnancy, had broken the spring while doing her Royal Canadian Women's Division Air Force Exercises on the sofa. She did them every evening, and was very diligent and disciplined about it; she followed them out of a book.

"You'd be dead wrong if you were sorry, Una, I mean that seriously. I'm being very sincere with you. The point is you're not the same person you used to be, is she, bunny?"

"She had these awfully conformist ideas, remember? Honest to God, Una, you were worse than Rosalie. Well, not *worse* really, but you acted just like Rosalie when we first knew her. Always mooning around us and toadying up. We couldn't *stand* it from her. I mean *there* was a type who had no individuality whatever. She didn't *believe* in individuality."

"And when we told her about it—you know, open and candid—she just got fresher and fresher. Don't look so upset, Una honey, *you're* not like that. She wasn't educable. The thing about you, Una, you've improved a lot because you're educable. You're on the brink of maturity, you could find yourself, your true métier, any day now—I mean, look at Mary, if you want an example—and all it would take to throw you off is for a guy like Organski to come along right about now and give you the business and tell you you ought to be one of these little housewife-types—"

"He didn't say anything like that," Una said slowly. Then, just as slowly, she yawned. She was really very tired.

"I nearly forgot. Here." She held out a package. "It's the liquid vitamins for Christina. Boris said they're awfully expensive if you have to buy them in the drugstore. He said when he left here he remembered where he could get a whole load of doctors' samples, you know, for free, and then he ran right over to the Woolworth's with them. That's what he met me for. To deliver them. I'm so collapsed I think I'll just sleep in my clothes. Could you shut the light off, please?"

Pang, went the spring, but Una didn't hear.

VI · After that Boris took to meeting Una outside the Woolworth's every night. At first she was astonished to see him there, leaning against the display windows and reading one of his medical books, waiting for her to come out; but he appeared so regularly that after the second week she began to look for him almost hopefully. The other clerks laughed and called out at him, as they passed, names like Totem Pole and Cigar Store Indian, and asked if he thought the place would fall in if he weren't around all the time to hold it up, and Boris always bowed comically but heartily to the fattest girls. That, he told Una, was a lesson to her: only fat girls were worth paying attention to. His object, he explained, was to fatten her up before he made her his mistress.

They always went to the same sandwich shop and Boris always bought her two thick sandwiches.

"Eat, don't talk," he said, and kept his head down among anatomical drawings until she was done. "I don't call that finished," he objected—that was if she left her crusts—and then he ordered her a chocolate malted milk, sometimes with an egg beaten into it. Meanwhile he studied and forgot his coffee until it was too cold to drink. He never took her home before midnight, but on the way—they always walked, even on the stormiest nights—he made up for his two hours' silence in the sandwich place by teasing without a stop. "Now promise, tomorrow I want a weight report. Without shoes, please, and in the nude, and on a reliable scale, try the one in the drugstore. I once had a mistress who was all skin and bones, like you, an experience I hope never to repeat. The points of her elbows made pinholes right through my best sheets. You should see those sheets today. In time the holes expanded to the size of washbasins, but you don't get to marvel at this phenomenon until I can observe the effects of ten pounds more in the clavicle area. A clavicle should not have such exaggerated visibility. The skeletal structure of the human body is not for public display except in the medical laboratory. My bedroom is not *that* sort of laboratory, my dear," but by then they were at the Chimeses' door.

"What'll I *tell* them?" Una whispered one night, in the middle of only her first sandwich.

"Eat, don't talk," said Boris.

"Boris!"

"Five minutes more. Just be quiet, my sweet, until I've done my gall bladder and liver. —Finish your crusts, there's a dear."

"Boris, I've *already* told Clement and Mary an awful lie. I told them the hardware supervisor extended my time by one hour."

Boris looked up from his book and scratched an ear. It happened to be Una's.

"Well, it was only because they're mad that I'm always getting home so late. I couldn't tell them it's for nothing. I *had* to lie."

"Aha," Boris said. "Thank you. I'm obliged to you. To Miss Meyer, Mr. Organski is nothing."

"Oh, Boris! Just *listen*. First I told them I was working this one hour overtime, and so then they wanted to know where the extra money was. Then I had to say *some*thing, so I said it was just plain overtime, and there wasn't any pay for it. And they didn't believe me! And now they want to know where I *go* after work. I don't know what to tell them, Boris."

"Naturally they haven't heard you're out with Organski? Naturally. 'I'm out with nothing' doesn't sound convincing."

"It's because I'm getting home too late, Boris. Really, couldn't we leave earlier? Couldn't we leave right now?"

"Before you've had your fortified malted milk? Never!"

"But it's ruining everything, I keep oversleeping. I overslept practically every morning this week and nobody got any breakfast, not even Christina, and later on she howled for hours, and Clement was so mad he couldn't do his chapter, and Mary said she was sick to her stomach in the library the whole day. She gets that way on an empty stomach. It's because I'm getting home too late, Boris."

"All right," Boris said. "We leave right now. Immediately. Will that satisfy you? It interferes with my studying, of course—that goes without saying—but if it satisfies you to interfere with my studying let's go. Organski's entire career may go up the flue, but Una Meyer must be satisfied. Mr. and Mrs. Chimes *told* me what a model of selfishness you are, I can't say I haven't been warned. Up with you. Come! Leave your crusts, please, we have no time for them. There will be no beverage tonight, madam," he yelled to the waitress.

"Oh, Boris, stop!" Una wailed. "I don't know *what* to do, honest I don't."

"Abandon fantasy. Tell Clement and Mary you're out with your lover. Excuse me. Your *prospective* lover—I'm afraid you're still several pounds short of realization of the fact, my dear. If you expose our liaison, you see, it will perhaps hint to them that you have an adumbration of a chimera of a life of your own."

"Boris, that's not the *point*," Una said, refusing even to smile.

"Aha. Clement's phrase exactly. You've mastered his intonation to the life, my dear. He spoke those very words to me, in that very tone, this very evening."

"You've seen *Clement?*" Una exclaimed.

"Only by chance. I intended to see Christina and he happened to be in the house. He was eating an apple at the time and comfortably reading the funnies. He said the funnies were not the point. Meanwhile I took a sampling of the poor child's sputum."

"Oh. Then she's worse," Una said.

"Dr. Chichester's having a peep at her in the morning—obviously a good man, he recognized Organski's gifts and gave him an A. That was last term. This term Una Meyer does not permit Organski to study. Oh, there won't be a fee, don't look so wild-eyed. Actually there *is* something wrong with your eyes, now that I observe them."

"What?" Una cried.

"They're half shut. Tell you what. Beginning tomorrow night, instead of fattening you here, I'll fatten you privately, in my own apartment. I have a little kitchen you'll find perfectly adequate for slicing baloney in. While I study you'll sleep. On one condition—that you avoid further puncturing my sheets with a randomly protruding bone. After which I'll walk you home."

"That won't solve anything," Una said gloomily.

"Ungrateful girl. Think of the Chimeses' going without breakfast! You'll have your duty sleep, won't you?"

"But what'll I tell Clement and Mary?"

"You'll tell them," Boris said peacefully, "the simple truth. That you were innocently slumbering in the bed of your lover."

VII · Boris was right about his sheets. They were terribly ragged. And his apartment was a calamity. The lease was handed on from one generation of students to another, year after year, and though everyone always left something behind, no one ever took anything away. The two rooms were full of useless objects, and the grease on the stove was as high as a finger. There was a television set that didn't work, a vacuum cleaner ditto, and, right in the middle of the tiny kitchen, a bureau stuffed with old underwear.

"My goodness," Una said, "hasn't this place ever been swept at all?"

"Long, long ago, my sweet, but only by the primeval Flood," Boris replied, and opened the refrigerator with a flourish. It was crammed with food.

"I feel awful," Una said. "I feel just so depressed about the whole thing, Boris, it's horrible. Clement and Mary are just sick about it."

"Eat, don't talk," Boris said. He settled himself at his desk. It stood at the foot of his unmade bed. The lamp had a red shade and his face looked pink under it. Una suddenly noticed how, when he lowered his head, the bulb of Boris's nose made a shadow over his mouth. He had a long, attractive nose, a bit thick at the tip, and long, stiff nostrils that stared downward like an extra pair of eyes. It was as though everything he said was uttered under surveillance.

"Itt, dunt tuck," Una mocked; she had begun not to mind his accent so much. "Do you have any olives?" It was a third-hand taste; Una had acquired it from the Chimeses, who had acquired it from Rosalie.

"In the closet. No, not that one, look in the one with my raincoat. There's a jar in the right pocket."

"I bet you spent the whole afternoon in the supermarket," Una accused, "and then you say you never get any time to study. These are green. Don't you have any black?"

"It doesn't matter, the fat content is nearly the same. —Oleo your bread, my dear, always oleo your bread."

"You can't imagine the atmosphere over there, Boris. Everybody's so upset. Clement's stopped work on his book. He doesn't think he'll ever finish it now, he says he's lost the thread. Boris?"

"No, dear, no conversation, please, I'm on the spleen tonight. The spleen is a very complicated organ."

"Boris, how long will Christina have to stay in the hospital?"

"Till Chichester lets her out. I suppose you forgot your toothbrush?"

"I brought it," Una said dejectedly. "I'm positive it's my fault she got sick in the first place."

"You're not a microscopic organism, my sweet. It can be proved incontrovertibly by the presence of your thirty-two teeth. Brush them, dear, and go to sleep right away or you won't wake up on time to go home. It's my duty to inform you that you're still five pounds avoirdupois short of spending the night."

But when Una got into Boris's bed he left his desk and started kissing her. She was rather surprised, because she was pretty sure he couldn't have progressed very far into his spleen.

"My luck," Boris said with his little croak. "For a mistress I have to pick a reader of the expurgated versions. Listen, my sweet, your Catullus was bowdlerized—the villains suppressed everything profitable, especially the best verbs. Now, hold the principal parts *so*," and he kissed her once more. And then Una was surprised all over again—it turned out she liked it. She liked it so much, in fact, that Boris finally had to give it up. "I don't want to keep you awake, my dear, or you won't be able to say you slept in Organski's bed. Well, Una," he finished, "anyhow I can tell you you're educable."

"That's what Clement and Mary always say," Una boasted, but dolefully. "Poor Mary. If Christina has to stay in the hospital for very long she won't get her thesis done on time. Dr. Chichester told them they'd better *be* in the hospital every day till the danger's over. Mary might even lose her degree. It's awful, that little perfect angel, all of a sudden such a fever and everything," and, rather earlier than they had expected to, they walked home to the Chimeses, in gloom over Christina.

When Una opened the door she saw a terrible sight. Clement and Mary were at war. Mary's left temple was bleeding. Clement's shirt was ripped across the back. Mary was dashing from room to room, spitting at things, and Clement ran after her. His shouts were violent and dirty. Mary spat on the tapestries, she fled from bookcase to bookcase, spitting on the shelves. She pulled down *The Princess Casamassima* and began tearing out handfuls of pages. Her hair fell down over her neck and her teeth blazed with spittle. "Damn it all," Mary said, "damn it all, *I* was away all day, *you* were the one who was always home—" "Crap on you, you're supposed to be the goddamn *mother*, aren't you?" "Derelict! Psychotic! Theologian!" Mary screamed, and for a moment a subtleness crept across her face. Then she whirled and seized a pile of records, trying to smash them with her shoe, but they were plastic and wouldn't break, so instead she hurled them in a black rain at Clement. Clement rushed at her shins and threw her over. They rolled and squirmed, pounding at one another—Clement was weeping, and a grid of long bright scratches was slowly bubbling red on Mary's arm. "Great, tag *me* with the blame, that's just the point, where *were* you, left her to a fool, a nincompoop, that girl doesn't know her thumb from her bum, an idiot—" "That's right, that's right, you've hit it," Mary yelled, "I left her with an idiot, I left her with you!"

Una was too stupefied to speak. A fight! Clement and Mary! Perfection!

She slipped out the door and raced down the street. Boris was trudging under the lamplight a block ahead of her. She ran and ran and caught up with him at last.

"Boris! I want to go back with you."

"Go home, Una."

"Boris, they're killing each other—"

"Unlikely. I eavesdropped for a second or so before boredom set in. Then I left. Go home."

"I can't go back there, Boris, they've *never* been like that. Boris, I want to stay with you tonight."

"I'm in no mood to collect rent, Una, go home to your friends."

"Boris," Una pleaded, "aren't you my friend? Be my friend, I can't go back there! They're crazy, they're insane, they're *attacking* each other—"

"Each other, no. An attack, yes. An attack of guilt. Go home, Una, they'll be all right," Boris said sadly. "Let me have a look at you. No lipstick, a convenience. Why don't you ever wear any?"

"I don't know," Una said. "Mary doesn't either."

"Mary's teeth stick out, she looks better without it. You should wear it," he said critically. He drew her away from the light and kissed her under a tree. It was a new kind of kiss.

"It wasn't like that in bed before," Una said wonderingly.

"Go home," Boris groaned, but it was half an hour before he let her go.

The house was quiet. A lava of wreckage spread everywhere. The Chimeses were waiting.

"About time," Clement greeted her. "Good morning, good morning."

Mary lay on the sofa face down. "We *saw* you come in before. We both saw you."

"We saw you slink out," Clement said. His chin was swollen and his mustache was a ruin. "You came in and you slunk right out again. We saw the whole thing."

"Christina's in the hospital and all Una Meyer can find to do is neck all night with a Bulgarian," Mary rasped into the upholstery. She shifted and sat up, and the bad spring snapped like the note of a bassoon.

"I'll be frank with you," Clement said. "Open and candid. We've been talking you over, Una. We've analyzed exactly what you've done."

"We've analyzed what you are."

"An exploiter," Clement said.

"Exploiter," said Mary. "Manipulator."

"When we asked you to come in halfies with us it was for your sake. Build up your ego and so forth. The Sorcerer's Apprentice, it turned out." Clement scowled. "We never dreamed you'd take over."

"You took over everything."

"The whole damn house."

"The books."

"The john."

"The records."

"The refrigerator."

"The baby," Mary said. "You had her out in the middle of blizzards, you were always practically suffocating her trying to shut her up—"

"She was abused," Clement said. "We depended on you and you abused the kid. You abused our good faith. You took over, that's all."

Una stared at the floor. A hassock had burst in the battle and there were peculiar cloud-bits stirring like little roaming mice.

"A matter of neglect," Mary said bitterly. "It began with Organski. After he started hanging around you could never keep your mind on anything. We told you he was no good."

"He's *good*," Una said. "If not for Boris nobody would ever've found out what was wrong with Christina, it would've been worse—"

"*Could* it be worse?" Mary asked.

"Never mind, bunny, don't try talking decency to her. He's set her against us, that's the point."

Una felt obscurely startled; she tasted salt. Then a wetness heated her nose, and she realized she had been crying all along.

"Isn't it a bit late for theatricals?" Mary said. "The least you can do is clean up the place. Clement's shirt's in little pieces."

"One thing you managed to do, my God, Rosalie at her worst never could. You even set the two of us against each *other*. Compared to you Rosalie was a goddamn saint."

Una put her arms behind her. "I know it's my fault. Boris said it wasn't. I mean about Christina. But it really is my fault, I know it is," and went on silently discharging tears.

"Maudlin!" Mary cried. "That's the worst thing about you, it's disgusting the way you like to go on like that, it's just masochism. She's so *humble* it's sickening, a born martyr, always got her neck stuck out for the persecutors. Look, if you want somebody to make you suffer, go find your pal Boris."

"Boris is good," Una repeated stupidly.

"He's not serious," Clement said. "These medical types never are. I know what you want out of him, but forget it. He's no damn good, whatever you say. Mary and I spotted it the first time we set eyes on him, but you knew better. You never listened to anything. We used to think something could be done with you, you could be salvaged, but the material turned out to be weak. You're in shreds, Una. That man will never marry you."

"She'll get what she deserves from that man," Mary said

"If he's as good as she thinks he'll give it to her good," Clement said; and because this was rather witty, Una saw him suddenly smile.

VIII · Early in the morning the Chimeses went to the hospital. Una couldn't go with them; they told her only the parents were allowed. She washed the breakfast dishes and scrubbed Mary's blood off the sofa and swept the living room and heaped together a pile of broken plunder. Then she tried to read a little. It seemed to her years had passed since she had read anything at all. No book could interest her. She mooned into the study, looking for Clement's manuscript.

There it was finally: under a mound of newspapers on the table he had made for Mary out of the bathroom door. The first page said

SOCIAL CANCER
A DIAGNOSIS IN VERSE
AND ANGER
By Clement Chimes, M.A.

There was no second page.

The day was long and tedious. Una could think of nothing worth doing. At six o'clock she would have to go back to the hardware counter, but there were hours before that. She walked out to Boris's, and of course he wasn't home.

A family of young cockroaches filed out of a crack between two boards and ducked their tall antennae over the sill. Una wished she had a key. Then she wished she could slide under the door like the cockroaches. She squatted on the floor in front of Boris's apartment and waited for his classes to be done. It grew dark in the corridor, and cold. "Oh Lord, a visitation," Boris muttered when he found her, and they nuzzled their way into bed and kissed there all afternoon. Una was late for work, but she felt warm and almost plump; her lips and cheeks and breasts and arms felt warm and golden. Boris's key was in her pocket.

The next evening the hardware supervisor gave her a warning for two latenesses in a row; it was easy to get girls these days, he said.

The Chimeses scarcely spoke to her. Their mood was strange. In the mornings they seemed to float out to the hospital, not with anxiety, but as though anxiety was over. They couldn't tell Una much about Christina. She was better, they murmured—she was definitely better. Boris, who kept in touch with Dr. Chichester, said nothing. Una was encouraged. Everyone struck her as optimistic—more than that, almost happy. The Chimeses' relief was clear. Boris rolled her all over his bed, laughing. By the end of the week she was fired, but the Chimeses only looked docile when Una told them she would have no money toward the rent.

She talked and talked to Boris. She talked to him about the Chimeses' queer enchanted gratitude. Day after day they passed through the hospital waiting rooms like scheming honeymooners. Afterward the nurses told how their heads were always close. They were noticed because they were beautiful and because they lived on candy bars. Their vigil left them not haggard but fresh and radiant. Una remembered how Mary had once, and more than once, praised the science of soil chemistry: it had more to contribute to the fortunes of the underdeveloped nations than bloodless jurisprudence could. And it came to her how Clement often spoke of traveling to a country where all the inhabitants practiced a totally unfamiliar religion, and how he always ended by twitting Una for throwing away her chance at diving into Turkey and the Koran. All along Mary had been bored and Clement jealous. They were relieved. They were glad to be interrupted. Fate had marred their perfect dedication and they did not despair. A brilliance stirred them. They were ready for something new.

By the beginning of the Chimeses' second hospital week Boris and Una were lovers in earnest, and in the middle of that same week Christina died. The sight of a small box handed down into a small ditch made Una think of a dog burying a bone. The young rabbi wore a crumpled bow tie. At the graveside he celebrated all students and intellectuals who do not neglect the duty of procreation—plainly it was his first funeral, and after it the Chimeses sold their books and left New Haven, and Una never saw them again.

IX · Sometimes she thought she read about them.
A headline would say WOMAN JOINS PEACE CORPS TO GIVE
HUSBAND SOME PEACE; it would be about a girl who went to
Tanganyika while her husband sat home in the quiet to
write a novel about corruption in the banking business, and
Una would hunt down the column avidly to see the names,
but it was always about someone else. Or she would hear of
a couple adopted by an Indian tribe and living right on the
reservation, teaching the elders Hochdeutsch and solid
geometry—it wasn't Clement and Mary, though. Once she
got wind of a young man who had left his wife, a beautiful
and dark-haired agronomist working in Burma, to enter a
Buddhist monastery, and she was positive this at last must
be the Chimeses, repaired and reconverted by fresh educa-
tions. But when the story was finally printed in *Time*, the
remarkable pair turned out to be Soviet citizens; they hailed
from Pinsk.

"Forget about them," Boris said, but she never could. She
was always expecting the Chimeses to jump out at her from
a newspaper, already famous.

"I've got their *card* catalogue, haven't I? What if they
want to reconstitute their library some day? They'll need
it."

"They're no good," Boris said.

"That's what they used to say about you."

"Two rights don't make a wrong."

"Ha ha," Una sneered. "They *were* wrong in one thing.
They swore you'd never marry me."

Boris sighed. "After all they had a point."

"No they didn't. They meant you'd never *want* to."

"I want to, Una," Boris said, and he asked her to marry
him for the thousandth time. "Why not? Why not? I don't

see why you won't say yes. Really, Una, what're you worrying about? Everything would be just the same as it is now."

"You're embarrassed," Una accused. "You're ashamed. Everybody knows about us and you can't stand it."

"That caps it. Now look. Let's go over it again, all right? *I'm* not the one who cares; the hospitals do. How do you think I'm going to get a decent internship anywhere? In a first-class clinic? Who's going to take me? Enough is enough. Let's get married, Una."

"Don't talk about everything being the same," Una said. "Everything's different already. *You're* not the same."

"Neither are you. You're a lot dumber than you used to be. And a bit of a shrew. You don't have a thought in your head any more. You fuss over grease, you fuss over dust—"

"I'm not as educated as you are," Una said meanly. "I gave up my education for the sake of the Phillips screwdriver and the Yale lock."

"I told you not to go back to that idiotic job."

"Who paid the bill to have the place fumigated? Who paid for the kitchen paint? And I notice you don't mind eating," Una said. "You're more interested in eating than you are in me anyhow. You always were. The only thing you ever liked about me was watching me eat."

"It's a lot less agonizing than watching you cook. Shrew," Boris said, "let's get married."

"No."

"Why the hell not? Finally and rationally, what've you got against it?"

"There's no education in it!" Una yelled.

"I don't want a mistress," Boris said, "I want a wife."

In the end—but this was years later, and how it came about, what letters were written, how often and how many, who introduced whom: all this was long forgotten—Boris did get a wife. When Una visited the Organskis ten years after their marriage, Boris was unrecognizable, except for the length of his nose; Una thought to herself that he looked like a long-nosed hippopotamus. His little boy, though only seven years old, seemed more like the medical student she remembered; he was arrogant and charming, and kept her laughing. Mrs. Organski was herself deliciously fat—but then she had always been fat, even in girlhood. She was newly widowed when Una got the idea that she would do nicely for Boris. Boris was now a psychiatrist. He had never stopped writing her his complicated, outrageous letters; he said he had finally come to understand that she was suffering from an ineradicable marriage-trauma. She had already been married vicariously; she had *lived* the Chimeses' marriage, she continued to believe in its perfection, and she was afraid she would fail to duplicate it. Now and again he offered to marry her in spite of everything.

Una finished her Ph.D. at a midwestern university; her old adviser and his wife and sons telegraphed an orchid. Her dissertation topic was "The Influence of the Greek Middle Voice on Latin Prosody," and it required no travel, foreign or internal. By a horrid coincidence she joined the faculty of a small college in Turkey, New York. All her colleagues were invincibly domesticated. They gave each other little teas and frequent dinner parties. Occasionally they invited some of the more intelligent teachers from the high school that bordered the campus. One of these turned out to be a Mrs. Orenstein, who taught social studies. Una and Mrs. Orenstein fell into one another's arms, and left the party early to reminisce in privacy. Mrs. Orenstein chafed her short fingers and told how Mr. Orenstein, a popular phys. ed. teacher, had been killed six months before in a terrible accident in the gym. Demonstrating a belly grind, he slipped off the parallel bars. The rest of the night they talked about the Chimeses. Mrs. Orenstein had heard from someone that Clement had become a dentist; an accountant from someone else; but she didn't know whether either was true. There was a rumor that Mary was with the State Department; another that Mary had become a nun and Clement a pimp for the Argentinean consul's brother-in-law. What was definite was that they lived in Washington; maybe they lived in Washington; they were both teaching astronomy at UCLA; they had no children; they had six girls and a boy; Mary was in prison; Clement was dead.

Finally Mrs. Orenstein asked Una why she had never married. Una thought the question rude and deflected it: "If you ever want to get married again, Rosalie, I have just the person. He'd like everything about you. Clement and Mary always used to say you were a good cook anyhow."

"I hated them," Rosalie said. "I hate them right now when I think about them, don't you?"

"I don't know," Una said. "I used to, but Boris mixed me up about them years ago. Just before I met Boris I was really hating them. I was a rotten hypocrite in those days. Then the baby died and they blamed me, so I started feeling sorry for them. The more Boris showed them up for selfish and shallow and all that, and not awfully bright after all, the more I began to see that they *had* something anyhow. I mean they kept themselves intact. They had *that*."

Rosalie snorted. "Anybody could see right through them."

"Well, what of it?" Una said. "It didn't matter. You could see through them and they were wonderful all the same, just *because* you could see through them. They were like a bubble that never broke, you could look right through and they kept on shining no matter what. They're the only persons I've ever known who stayed the same from start to finish."

"I don't follow any of that," Rosalie said. "Who's this Boris?"

Una laughed furiously. "Rosalie, Rosalie, aren't you listening? Boris is your second husband."

She waited a decade before she dared to visit them; she was forty-two years old. She had trouble with her gums, had lost some teeth, and wore movable bridges. "Has anybody ever heard anything about the Chimeses?" No one had.

"Ding dong," said the new Organski daughter, and everyone smiled.

Oddly enough the visit was a success. She observed the Organskis' marriage. They had a full and heavy table, and served three desserts: first pudding, then fruit, then cake and tea. The two children would plainly never turn out to be extraordinary. Boris's accent was as bad as ever. Rosalie let the dust build; she quarreled with all her cleaning women. The house held no glory and no wars.

Rosalie asked Una to come again, and she accepted, but only with her lips. Inwardly she refused. It wasn't that she any longer resented imperfection, but it seemed to her unendurable that her education should go on and on and on.

(1964)

Usurpation
(Other People's Stories)

Occasionally a writer will encounter a story that is his, yet is not his. I mean, by the way, a writer of *stories*, not one of these intelligences that analyze society and culture, but the sort of ignorant and acquisitive being who moons after magical tales. Such a creature knows very little: how to tie a shoelace, when to go to the store for bread, and the exact stab of a story that belongs to him, and to him only. But sometimes it happens that somebody else has written the story first. It is like being robbed of clothes you do not yet own. There you sit, in the rapt hall, seeing the usurper on the stage caressing the manuscript that, in its deepest turning, was meant to be yours. He is a transvestite, he is wearing your own hat and underwear. It seems unjust. There is no way to prevent him.

You may wonder that I speak of a hall rather than a book. The story I refer to has not yet been published in a book, and the fact is I heard it read aloud. It was read by the author himself. I had a seat in the back of the hall, with a much younger person pressing the chair-arms on either side of me, but by the third paragraph I was blind and saw nothing. By the fifth paragraph I recognized my story—knew it to be mine, that is, with the same indispensable familiarity I have for this round-flanked left-side molar my tongue admires. I think of it, in all that waste and rubble amid gold dental crowns, as my pearl.

The story was about a crown—a mythical one, made of silver. I do not remember its title. Perhaps it was simply called "The Magic Crown." In any event, you will soon read it in its famous author's new collection. He is, you may be sure, very famous, so famous that it was startling to see he was a real man. He wore a conventional suit and tie, a conventional haircut and conventional eyeglasses. His whitening mustache made him look conventionally distinguished. He was not at all as I had expected him to be—small and astonished, like his heroes.

This time the hero was a teacher. In the story he was always called "the teacher," as if how one lives is what one is.

The teacher's father is in the hospital, a terminal case. There is no hope. In an advertisement the teacher reads about a wonder-curer, a rabbi who can work miracles. Though a rational fellow and a devout skeptic, in desperation he visits the rabbi and learns that a cure can be effected by the construction of a magical silver crown, which costs nearly five hundred dollars. After it is made the rabbi will give it a special blessing and the sick man will recover. The teacher pays and in a vision sees a glowing replica of the marvelous crown. But afterward he realizes that he has been mesmerized.

Furiously he returns to the rabbi's worn-out flat to demand his money. Now the rabbi is dressed like a rich dandy. "I telephoned the hospital and my father is still sick." The rabbi chides him— he must give the crown time to work. The teacher insists that the crown he paid for be produced. "It cannot be seen," says the rabbi, "it must be believed in, or the blessing will not work."

The teacher and the rabbi argue bitterly. The rabbi calls for faith, the teacher for his stolen money. In the heart of the struggle the teacher confesses with a terrible cry that he has really always hated his father anyway. The next day the father dies.

.   .   .

With a single half-archaic word the famous writer pressed out the last of the sick man's breath: he "expired."

Forgive me for boring you with plot-summary. I know there is nothing more tedious, and despise it myself. A rabbi whose face I have not made you see, a teacher whose voice remains a shadowy moan: how can I burn the inside of your eyes with these? But it is not my story, and therefore not my responsibility. I did not invent any of it.

From the platform the famous writer explained that the story was a gift, he too had not invented it. He took it from an account in a newspaper—which one he would not tell: he sweated over fear of libel. Cheats and fakes always hunt themselves up in stories, sniffing out twists, insults, distortions, transfigurations, all the drek of the imagination. Whatever's made up they grab, thick as lawyers against the silky figurative. Still, he swore it really happened, just like that—a crook with his crooked wife, calling himself rabbi, preying on gullible people, among them educated men, graduate students even; finally they arrested the fraud and put him in jail.

Instantly, the famous writer said, at the smell of the word "jail," he knew the story to be his.

This news came to me with a pang. The silver crown given away free, and where was I?—I who am pocked with newspaper-sickness, and hunch night after night (it pleases me to read the morning papers after midnight) catatonically fixed on shipping lists, death columns, lost wallets, maimings, muggings, explosions, hijackings, bombs, while the unwashed dishes sough thinly all around.

It has never occurred to me to write about a teacher; and as for rabbis, I can make up my own craftily enough. You may ask, then, what precisely in this story attracted me. And not simply attracted: seized me by the lung and declared itself my offspring—a changeling in search of its natural mother. Do not mistake me: had I only had access to a newspaper that crucial night (the *Post*, the *News*, the *Manchester Guardian*, *St. Louis Post-Dispatch*, *Boston Herald-Traveler*, ah, which, which? and where was I? in a bar? never; buying birth control pills in the drugstore? I am a believer in fertility; reading, God forbid, a *book?*), my own story would have been less logically decisive. Perhaps the sick father would have recovered. Perhaps the teacher would not have confessed to hating his father. I might have caused the silver crown to astonish even the rabbi himself. Who knows what I might have sucked out of those swindlers! The point is I would have fingered out the magical parts.

Magic—I admit it—is what I lust after. And not ordinary magic, which is what one expects of pagan peoples; their religions declare it. After all, half the world asserts that once upon a time God became a man, and moreover that whenever a priest in sacral ceremony wills it, that same God-man can climb into a little flat piece of unleavened bread. For most people nowadays it is only the *idea* of a piece of bread turning into God—but is that any better? As for me, I am drawn not to the symbol, but to the absolute magic act. I am drawn to what is forbidden.

Forbidden. The terrible Hebrew word for it freezes the tongue—*asur*; Jewish magic. Trembling, we have heard in Deuteronomy the No that applies to any slightest sniff of occult disclosure: how mighty is Moses, peering down the centuries into the endlessness of this allure! Astrologists, wizards and witches: *asur*. The Jews have no magic. For us bread may not tumble into body. Wine is wine, death is death.

And yet with what prowess we have crept down the centuries after amulets, and hidden countings of letters, and the silver crown that heals: so it is after all nothing to marvel at that my own, my beloved, subject should be the preternatural—everything anti-Moses, all things blazing with their own wonder. I long to be one of the ordinary peoples, to give up our agnostic God whom even the word "faith" insults, who cannot be imagined in any form, whom the very hope of imagining offends, who is without body and cannot enter body . . . oh, why can we not have a magic God like other peoples?

Some day I will take courage and throw over being a Jew, and then I will make a little god, a silver godlet, in the shape of a crown, which will stop death, resurrect fathers and uncles; out of its royal points gardens will burst. —That story! Mine! Stolen! I considered: was it possible to leap up on the stage with a living match and burn the manuscript on the spot, freeing the crown out of the finished tale, restoring it once more to a public account in the press? But no. Fire, even the little humble wobble of a match, is too powerful a magic in such a place, among such gleaming herds. A conflagration of souls out of lust for a story! I feared so terrible a spell. All the same, he would own a carbon copy, or a photographic copy: such a man is meticulous about the storage-matter of his brain. A typewriter is a volcano. Who can stop print?

If I owned a silver godlet right now I would say: Almighty small Crown, annihilate that story; return, return the stuff of it to me.

A peculiar incident. Just as the famous writer came to the last word—"expired"—I saw the face of a goat. It was thin, white, blurry-eyed; a scraggly fur beard hung from its chin. Attached to the beard was a transparent voice, a voice like a whiteness—but I ought to explain how I came just then to be exposed to it. I was leaning against the wall of that place. The fading hiss of "expired" had all at once fevered me; I jumped from my seat between the two young people. Their perspiration had dampened the chair-arms, and the chill of their sweat, combined with the hotness of my greed for this magic story which could not be mine, turned my flesh to a sort of vapor. I rose like a heated gas, feeling insubstantial, and went to press my head against the cold side wall along the aisle. My brain was all gas, it shuddered with envy. Expired! How I wished to write a story containing that unholy sound! How I wished it was I who had come upon the silver crown. . . . I must have looked like an usher, or in some fashion a factotum of the theater, with my skull drilled into the wall that way.

In any case I was taken for an official: as someone in authority who lolls on the job.

The goat-face blew a breath deep into my throat.

"I have stories. I want to give him stories."

"*What* do you want?"

"Him. Arrange it, can't you? In the intermission, what d'you say?"

I pulled away; the goat hopped after me.

"How? When?" said the goat. "Where?" His little beard had a tremor. "If he isn't available here and now, tell me his mailing address. I need criticism, advice, I need help—"

We become what we are thought to be; I became a factotum.

I said pompously, "You should be ashamed to pursue the famous. Does he know you?"

"Not exactly. I'm a cousin—"

"*His* cousin?"

"No. That rabbi's wife. She's an old lady, my mother's uncle was her father. We live in the same neighborhood."

"What rabbi?"

"The one in the papers. The one he swiped the story from."

"That doesn't oblige him to read you. You expect too much," I said. "The public has no right to a writer's private mind. Help from high places doesn't come like manna. His time is precious, he has better things to do." All this, by the way, was quotation. A famous writer—not this one—to whom I myself sent a story had once stung me with these words; so I knew how to use them.

"Did he say you could speak for him?" sneered the goat. "Fame doesn't cow me. Even the famous bleed."

"Only when pricked by the likes of you," I retorted. "Have you been published?"

"I'm still young."

"Poets before you died first and published afterward. Keats was twenty-six, Shelley twenty-nine, Rimbaud—"

"I'm like these, I'll live forever."

"Arrogant!"

"Let the famous call me that, not you."

"At least I'm published," I protested; so my disguise fell. He saw I was nothing so important as an usher, only another unknown writer in the audience.

"Do *you* know him?" he asked.

"He spoke to me once at a cocktail party."

"Would he remember your name?"

"Certainly," I lied. The goat had speared my dignity.

"Then take only one story."

"Leave the poor man alone."

"*You* take it. Read it. If you like it—look, only if you like it!—give it to him for me."

"He won't help you."

"Why do you think everyone is like you?" he accused— but he seemed all at once submerged, as if I had hurt him.

He shook out a vast envelope, pulled out his manuscript, and spitefully began erasing something. Opaque little tears clustered on his eyelashes. Either he was weeping or he was afflicted with pus. "Why do you think I don't deserve some attention?"

"Not of the great."

"Then let me at least have yours," he said.

The real usher just then came like a broom. Back! Back! Quiet! Don't disturb the reading! Before I knew it I had been swept into my seat. The goat was gone, and I was clutching the manuscript.

The fool had erased his name.

That night I read the thing. You will ask why. The newspaper was thin, the manuscript fat. It smelled of stable: a sort of fecal stink. But I soon discovered it was only the glue he had used to piece together parts of corrected pages. An amateur job.

If you are looking for magic now, do not. This was no work to marvel at. The prose was not bad, but not good either. There are young men who write as if the language were an endless bolt of yard goods—you snip off as much as you need for the length of fiction you require: one turn of the loom after another, everything of the same smoothness, the texture catches you up nowhere.

I have said "fiction." It was not clear to me whether this was fiction or not. The title suggested it was: "A Story of Youth and Homage." But the narrative was purposefully inconclusive. Moreover, the episodes could be interpreted on several "levels." Plainly it was not just a story, but meant something much more, and even that "much more" itself meant much more. This alone soured me; such techniques are learned in those hollowed-out tombstones called Classes in Writing. In my notion of these things, if you want to tell a story you tell it. I am against all these masks and tricks of metaphor and fable. That is why I am attracted to magical tales: they mean what they say; in them miracles are not symbols, they are conditional probabilities.

The goat's story was realistic enough, though self-conscious. In perfectly ordinary, mainly trite, English it pretended to be incoherent. That, as you know, is the fashion.

I see you are about to put these pages down, in fear of another plot-summary. I beg you to wait. Trust me a little. I will get through it as painlessly as possible—I promise to abbreviate everything. Or, if I turn out to be long-winded, at least to be interesting. Besides, you can see what risks I am taking. I am unfamiliar with the laws governing plagiarism, and here I am, brazenly giving away stories that are not rightfully mine. Perhaps one day the goat's story will be published and acclaimed. Or perhaps not: in either case he will recognize his plot as I am about to tell it to you, and what furies will beat in him! What if, by the time *this* story is published, at this very moment while you are reading it, I am on my back in some filthy municipal dungeon? Surely so deep a sacrifice should engage your forgiveness.

Then let us proceed to the goat's plot:

An American student at a yeshiva in Jerusalem is unable to concentrate. He is haunted by worldly desires; in reality he has come to Jerusalem not for Torah but out of ambition. Though young and unpublished, he already fancies himself to be a writer worthy of attention. Then why not the attention of the very greatest?

It happens that there lives in Jerusalem a writer who one day will win the most immense literary prize on the planet. At the time of the story he is already an old man heavy with fame, though of a rather parochial nature; he has not yet been to Stockholm—it is perhaps two years before the Nobel Prize turns him into a mythical figure. ["Turns him into a mythical figure" is an excellent example of the goat's prose, by the way.] But the student is prescient, and fame is fame. He composes a postcard:

> There are only two
> religious writers in the world.
> You are one and I am
> the other. I will come to visit you.

It is true that the old man is religious. He wears a skullcap, he threads his tales with strands of the holy phrases. And he cannot send anyone away from his door. So when the student appears, the old writer invites him in for a glass of tea, though homage fatigues him; he would rather nap.

The student confesses that his own ambitiousness has brought him to the writer's feet: he too would wish one day to be revered as the writer himself is revered.

—I wish, says the old writer, I had been like you in my youth. I never had the courage to look into the face of anyone I admired, and I admired so many! But they were all too remote; I was very shy. I wish now I had gone to see them, as you have come to see me.

—Whom did you admire most? asks the student. In reality he has no curiosity about this or anything else of the kind, but he recognizes that such a question is vital to the machinery of praise. And though he has never read a word the old man has written, he can smell all around him, even in the old man's trousers, the smell of fame.

—The Rambam, answers the old man. —Him I admired more than anyone.

—Maimonides? exclaims the student. —But how could you visit Maimonides?

—Even in my youth, the old man assents, the Rambam had already been dead for several hundred years. But even if he had not been dead, I would have been too shy to go and see him. For a shy young man it is relieving to admire someone who is dead.

—Then to become like you, the student says meditatively, it is necessary to be shy?

—Oh yes, says the old man. —It is necessary to be shy. The truest ambition is hidden in shyness. All ambitiousness is hidden. If you want to usurp my place you must not show it, or I will only hang to it all the more tightly. You must always walk with your head down. You must be a true *ba'al ga'avah.*

—A *ba'al ga'avah?* cries the student. —But you contradict yourself! Aren't we told that the *ba'al ga'avah* is the man whom God most despises? The self-righteous self-idolator? It's written that him alone God will cause to perish. Sooner than a murderer!

It is plain that the young man is in good command of the sources; not for nothing is he a student at the yeshiva. But he is perplexed, rattled. —How can I be like you if you tell me to be a *ba'al ga'avah?* And why would you tell me to be such a thing?

—The *ba'al ga'avah,* explains the writer, is a supplanter: the man whose arrogance is godlike, whose pride is like a tower. He is the one who most subtly turns his gaze downward to the ground, never looking at what he covets. I myself was never cunning enough to be a genuine *ba'al ga'avah;* I was always too timid for it. It was never necessary for me to feign shyness, I was naturally like that. But you are not. So you must invent a way to become a genuine *ba'al ga'avah,* so audacious and yet so ingenious that you will fool God and will live.

The student is impatient. —How does God come into this? We're talking only of ambition.

—Of course. Of *serious* ambition, however. You recall: "All that is not Torah is levity." This is the truth to be found at the end of every incident, even this one. —You see, the old man continues, my place can easily be taken. A blink, and it's yours. I will not watch over it if I forget that someone is after it. But you must make me forget.

—How? asks the student, growing cold with greed.

—By never coming here again.

—It's a joke!

—And then I will forget you. I will forget to watch over my place. And then, when I least look for it to happen, you will come and steal it. You will be so quiet, so shy, so ingenious, so audacious, I will never suspect you.

—A nasty joke! You want to get rid of me! It's mockery, you forget what it is to be young. In old age everything is easier, nothing burns inside you.

But meanwhile, inside the student's lungs, and within the veins of his wrists, a cold fog shivers.

—Nothing burns? Yes; true. At the moment, for instance, I covet nothing more lusty than my little twilight nap. I always have it right now.

—They say (the student is as cold now as a frozen path, all his veins are paths of ice), they say you're going to win the Nobel Prize! For literature!

—When I nap I sleep dreamlessly. I don't dream of such things. Come, let me help you cease to covet.

—It's hard for me to keep my head down! I'm young, I want what you have, I want to be like you!

Here I will interrupt the goat's story to apologize. I would not be candid if I did not confess that I am rewriting it; I am almost making it my own, and that will never do for an act of plagiarism. I don't mean only that I have set it more or less in order, and taken out the murk. That is only by the way. But, by sticking to what one said and what the other answered, I have broken my promise; already I have begun to bore you. Boring! Oh, the goat's story was boring! Philosophic stories make excellent lullabies.

So, going on with my own version (I hate stories with ideas hidden in them), I will spring out of paraphrase and invent what the old man does.

Right after saying "Let me help you cease to covet," he gets up and, with fuzzy sleepy steps, half-limps to a table covered by a cloth that falls to the floor. He separates the parts of the cloth, and now the darkness underneath the table takes him like a tent. In he crawls, the flaps cling, his rump makes a bulge. He calls out two words in Hebrew: *ohel shalom!* and backs out, carrying with him a large black box. It looks like a lady's hat box.

"An admirer gave me this. Only not an admirer of our own time. A predecessor. I had it from Tchernikhovsky. The poet. I presume you know his work?"

"A little," says the student. He begins to wish he had boned up before coming.

"Tchernikhovsky was already dead when he brought me this," the old man explains. "One night I was alone, sitting right there—where you are now. I was reading Tchernikhovsky's most famous poem, the one to the god Apollo. And quite suddenly there was Tchernikhovsky. He disappointed me. He was a completely traditional ghost, you could see right through him to the wall behind. This of course made it difficult to study his features. The wall behind—you can observe for yourself—held a bookcase, so where his nose appeared to be I could read only the title of a Tractate of the Mishnah. A ghost can be seen mainly in outline, unfortunately, something like an artist's charcoal sketch, only instead of the blackness of charcoal, it is the narrow brilliance of a very fine white light. But what he carried was palpable, even heavy—this box. I was not at all terror-stricken, I can't tell you why. Instead I was bemused by the kind of picture he made against the wall—'modern,' I would have called it then, but probably there are new words for that sort of thing now. It reminded me a little of a collage: one kind of material superimposed on another kind which is utterly different. One order of creation laid upon another. Metal on tissue. Wood on hide. In this case it was a three-dimensional weight superimposed on a line—the line, or luminous congeries of lines, being Tchernikhovsky's hands, ghost hands holding a real box."

The student stares at the box. He waits like a coat eager to be shrunk.

"The fact is," continues the old writer, "I have never opened it. Not that I'm not as inquisitive as the next mortal. Perhaps more so. But it wasn't necessary. There is something about the presence of an apparition which satisfies all curiosity forever—the deeper as well as the more superficial sort. For one thing, a ghost will tell you everything, and all at once. A ghost may *look* artistic, but there is no finesse to it, nothing indirect or calculated, nothing suggesting *raffinement*. It is as if everything gossamer had gone simply into the stuff of it. The rest is all grossness. Or else Tchernikhovsky himself, even when alive and writing, had a certain clumsiness. This is what I myself believe. All that pantheism and earth-worship! That pursuit of the old gods of Canaan! He thickened his tongue with clay. All pantheists are fools. Likewise trinitarians and gnostics of every kind. How can a piece of creation be its own Creator?

"Still, his voice had rather a pretty sound. To describe it is to be obliged to ask you to recall the sound of prattle: a baby's purr, only shaped into nearly normal cognitive speech. A most pleasing combination. He told me that he was reading me closely in Eden and approved of my stories. He had, he assured me, a number of favorites, but best of all he liked a quite short tale—no more than a notebook sketch, really—about why the Messiah will not come.

"In this story the Messiah is ready to come. He enters a synagogue and prepares to appear at the very moment he hears the congregation recite the 'I believe.' He stands there and listens, waiting to make himself visible on the last syllable of the verse 'I believe in the coming of the Messiah, and even if he tarry I will await his coming every day.' He leans against the Ark and listens, listens and leans—all the time he is straining his ears. The fact is he can hear nothing: the congregation buzzes with its own talk—hats, mufflers, business, wives, appointments, rain, lessons, the past, next week . . . the prayer is obscured, all its syllables are drowned in dailiness, and the Messiah retreats; he has not heard himself summoned.

"This, Tchernikhovsky's ghost told me, was my best story. I was at once suspicious. His baby-voice hinted at ironies, I caught a tendril of sarcasm. It was clear to me that what he liked about this story was mainly its climactic stroke: that the Messiah is prevented from coming. I had written to lament the tarrying of the Messiah; Tchernikhovsky, it seemed, took satisfaction exactly in what I mourned. 'Look here,' he tinkled at me—imagine a crow linked to a delicious little gurgle, and the whole sense of it belligerent as a prize-fighter and coarse as an old waiter—'now that I'm dead, a good quarter-century of deadness under my dust, I've concluded that I'm entirely willing to have you assume my eminence. For one thing, I've been to Sweden, pulled strings with some deceased but still influential Academicians, and arranged for you to get the Nobel Prize in a year or two. Which is beyond what I ever got for myself. But I'm aware this won't interest you as much as a piece of eternity right here in Jerusalem, so I'm here to tell you you can have it. You can'—he had a babyish way of repeating things—'assume my eminence.'

"You see what I mean about grossness. I admit I was equally coarse. I answered speedily and to the point. I refused.

" 'I understand you,' he said. 'You don't suppose I'm pious enough, or not pious in the right way. I don't meet your yeshiva standards. Naturally not. You know I used to be a doctor, I was attracted to biology, which is to say to dust. Not spiritual enough for you! My Zionism wasn't of the soul, it was made of real dirt. What I'm offering you is something tangible. Have some common sense and take it. It will do for you what the Nobel Prize can't. Open the box and put on whatever's inside. Wear it for one full minute and the thing will be accomplished.' "

"For God's sake, what *was* it?" shrieks the student, shriveling into his blue city-boy shirt. With a tie: and in Jerusalem! (The student is an absurdity, a crudity. But of course I've got to have him; he's left over from the goat's story, what else am I to do?)

"Inside the box," replies the old writer, "was the most literal-minded thing in the world. From a ghost I expected as much. The whole idea of a ghost is a literal-minded conception. I've used ghosts in my own stories, naturally, but they've always had a real possibility, by which I mean an ideal possibility: Elijah, the True Messiah. . . ."

"For God's sake, the box!"

"The box. Take it. I give it to you."

"What's in it?"

"See for yourself."

"Tell me first. Tchernikhovsky told *you.*"

"That's a fair remark. It contains a crown."

"What kind of crown?"

"Made of silver, I believe."

"*Real* silver?"

"I've never looked on it, I've explained this. I *refused* it."

"Then why give it to me?"

"Because it's meant for that. When a writer wishes to usurp the place and power of another writer, he simply puts it on. I've explained this already."

"But if I wear it I'll become like Tchernikhovsky—"

"No, no, like me. Like me. It confers the place and power of the giver. And it's what you want, true? To be like me?"

"But this isn't what you advised a moment ago. *Then* you said to become arrogant, a *ba'al ga'avah,* and to conceal it with shyness—"

(Quite so. A muddle in the plot. That was the goat's story, and it had no silver crown in it. I am still stuck with these leftovers that cause seams and cracks in my own version. I will have to mend all this somehow. Be patient. I will manage it. Pray that I don't bungle it.)

"Exactly," says the old writer. "That's the usual way. But if you aren't able to feign shyness, what is necessary is a short cut. I warned you it would demand audacity and ingenuity. What I did not dare to do, you must have the courage for. What I turned down you can raise up. I offer you the crown. You will see what a short cut it is. Wear it and immediately you become a *ba'al ga'avah.* Still, I haven't yet told you how I managed to get rid of Tchernikhovsky's ghost. Open the box, put on the crown, and I'll tell you."

The student obeys. He lifts the box onto the table. It

seems light enough, then he opens it, and at the first thrust of his hand into its interior it disintegrates, flakes off into dust, is blown off at a breath, consumed by the first alien molecule of air, like something very ancient removed from the deepest clay tomb and unable to withstand the corrosive stroke of light.

But there, in the revealed belly of the vanished box, is the crown.

It appears to be made of silver, but it is heavier than any earthly silver—it is heavy, heavy, heavy, dense as a meteorite. Puffing and struggling, the student tries to raise it up to his head. He cannot. He cannot lift even a corner of it. It is weighty as a pyramid.

"It won't budge."

"It will after you pay for it."

"You didn't say anything about payment!"

"You're right. I forgot. But you don't pay in money. You pay in a promise. You have to promise that if you decide you don't want the crown you'll take it off immediately. Otherwise it's yours forever."

"I promise."

"Good. Then put it on."

And now lightly, lightly, oh so easily as if he lifted a straw hat, the student elevates the crown and sets it on his head.

"There. You are like me. Now go away."

And oh so lightly, lightly, as easily as if the crown were a cargo of helium, the student skips through Jerusalem. He runs! He runs into a bus, a joggling mob crushed together, everyone recognizes him, even the driver: he is praised, honored, young women put out their hands to touch his collar, they pluck at his pants, his fly unzips and he zips it up again, oh fame! He gets off the bus and runs to his yeshiva.

Crowds on the sidewalk, clapping. So this is what it feels like! He flies into the yeshiva like a king. Formerly no one blinked at him, the born Jerusalemites scarcely spoke to him, but now! It is plain they have all read him. He hears a babble of titles, plots, characters, remote yet familiar—look, he thinks, the crown has supplied me with a ready-made bibliography. He reaches up to his head to touch it: a flash of cold. Cold, cold, it is the coldest silver on the planet, a coldness that stabs through into his brain. Frost encases his brain, inside his steaming skull he hears more titles, more plots, names of characters, scholars, wives, lovers, ghosts, children, beggars, villages, candlesticks—what a load he carries, what inventions, what a teeming and a boiling, stories, stories, stories! His own; yet not his own. The Rosh Yeshiva comes down the stairs from his study: the Rosh Yeshiva, the Head, a bony miniaturized man grown almost entirely inward and upward into a spectacular dome, a brow shaped like the front of an academy, hollowed-out temples for porticoes, a resplendent head with round dead-end eye-glasses as denying as bottle-bottoms and curl-scribbled beard and small attachments of arms and little antlike legs thin as hairs; and the Rosh Yeshiva, who has never before let fall a syllable to this obscure tourist-pupil from America, suddenly cries out the glorious blessing reserved for finding oneself in the presence of a sage: Blessed are You, O God, Imparter of wisdom to those who fear Him! And the student in his crown understands that there now cleave to his name sublime parables interpreting the divine purpose, and he despairs, he is afraid, because suppose he were obliged to write one this minute? Suppose these titles clamoring all around him are only empty pots, and he must fill them up with stories? He runs from the yeshiva, elbows out, scattering admirers and celebrants, and makes for the alley behind the kitchen—no one ever goes there, only the old cats who scavenge in the trash barrels. But behind him—crudely sepulchral footsteps, like thumps inside a bucket, he runs, he looks back, he runs, he stops—Tchernikhovsky's ghost! From the old writer's description he can identify it easily. "A mistake," chimes the ghost, a pack of bells, "it wasn't for you."

"What!" screams the student.

"Give it back."

"What!"

"The crown," pursues the baby-purr voice of Tchernikhovsky's ghost. "I never meant for that old fellow to give it away."

"He said it was all right."

"He tricked you."

"No he didn't."

"He's sly sly sly."

"He said it would make me just like him. And I am."

"No."

"Yes!"

"Then predict the future."

"In two years, the Nobel Prize for Literature!"

"For him, not for you."

"But I'm *like* him."

" 'Like' is not the same as the same. You want to be the same? Look in the window."

The student looks into the kitchen window. Inside, among cauldrons, he can see the roil of the students in their caps, spinning here and there, in the pantry, in the Passover dish closet even, past a pair of smoky vats, in search of the fled visitor who now stares and stares until his concentration alters seeing; and instead of looking behind the pane, he follows the light on its surface and beholds a reflection. An old man is also looking into the window; the student is struck by such a torn rag of a face. Strange, it cannot be

Tchernikhovsky: he is all web and wraith; and anyhow a ghost has no reflection. The old man in the looking-glass window is wearing a crown. A silver crown!

"You see?" tinkles the ghost. "A trick!"

"I'm old!" howls the student.

"Feel in your pocket."

The student feels. A vial.

"See? Nitroglycerin."

"What is this, are you trying to blow me up?"

Again the small happy soaring of the infant's grunt. "I remind you that I am a physician. When you are seized by a pulling, a knocking, a burning in the chest, a throb in the elbow-crook, swallow one of these tablets. In coronary insufficiency it relaxes the artery."

"Heart failure! Will I die? Stop! I'm young!"

"With those teeth? All gums gone? That wattle? Dotard! Bag!"

The student runs; he remembers his perilous heart; he slows. The ghost thumps and chimes behind. So they walk, a procession of two, a very old man wearing a silver crown infinitely cold, in his shadow a ghost made all of lit spiderthread, giving out now and then with baby's laughter and odd coarse curses patched together from Bible phrases; together they scrape out of the alley onto the boulevard—an oblivious population there.

"My God! No one knows me. Why don't they know me here?"

"Who should know you?" says Tchernikhovsky.

"In the bus they yelled out dozens of book titles. In the streets! The Rosh Yeshiva said the blessing for seeing a sage!"

But now in the bus the passengers are indifferent; they leap for seats; they snore in cozy spots standing up, near poles; and not a word. Not a gasp, not a squeal. Not even a pull on the collar. It's all over! A crown but no king.

"It's stopped working," says the student, mournful.

"The crown? Not on your life."

"Then you're interfering with it. You're jamming it up."

"That's more like the truth."

"Why are you following me?"

"I don't like misrepresentation."

"You mean you don't like magic."

"They're the same thing."

"Go away!"

"I never do that."

"*He* got rid of you."

"Sly sly sly. He did it with a ruse. You know how? He refused the crown. He took it but he hid it away. No one ever refused it before. Usurper! Coveter! *Ba'al ga'avah!* That's what he is."

The student protests, "But he *gave* me the crown. 'Let me help you cease to covet,' that's exactly what he said, why do you call him *ba'al ga'avah?*"

"And himself? *He's* ceased to covet, is that it? That's what you think? You think he doesn't churn saliva over the Nobel Prize? Ever since I told him they were speculating about the possibility over at the Swedish Academicians' graveyard? Day and night that's all he dreams of. He loves his little naps, you know why? To sleep, perchance to dream. He imagines himself in a brand-new splendiferous bow-tie, rear end trailing tails, wearing his skullcap out of public arrogance, his old wife up there with him dressed to the hobbledorfs—in Stockholm, with the King of Sweden! That's what he sees, that's what he dreams, he can't work, he's in a fever of coveting. You think it's different when you're old?"

"I'm not old!" the student shouts. A willful splinter, he peels himself from the bus. Oh, frail, his legs are straw, the dry knees wrap close like sheaves, he feels himself pouring out, sand from a sack. Old!

Now they are in front of the writer's house. "Age makes no matter," says the ghost, "the same, the same. Ambition levels, lust is unitary. Lust you can always count on. I'm not speaking of the carnal sort. Carnality's a brevity—don't compare wind with mountains! But lust! Teetering on the edge of the coffin there's lust. After mortality there's lust, I guarantee you. In Eden there's nothing but lust." The ghost raps on the door—with all his strength, and his strength is equal to a snowflake. Silence, softness. "Bang on the thing!" he commands, self-disgusted; sometimes he forgets he is, incorporeal.

The student obeys, shivering; he is so cold now his three or six teeth clatter like chinaware against a waggling plastic bridge anchored in nothing, his ribs shake in his chest, his spine vibrates without surcease. And what of his heart? Inside his pocket he clutches the vial.

The old writer opens up. His fists are in his eyes.

"We woke you, did we?" gurgles Tchernikhovsky's ghost. "You!"

"Me," says the ghost, satisfied. *"Ba'al ga'avah!* Spiteful! You foisted the crown on a kid."

The old writer peers. "Where?"

The ghost sweeps the student forward. "I did him the service of giving him long life. Instantly. Why wait for a good thing?"

"I don't want it! Take it back!" the student cries, snatching at the crown on his head; but it stays on. "You said I could give it back if I don't want it any more!"

Again the old writer peers. "Ah. You keep your promise. So does the crown."

"What do you mean?"

"It promised you acclaim. But it generates this pest. Everything has its price."

"Get rid of it!"

"To get rid of the ghost you have to get rid of the crown."

"All right! Here it is! Take it back! It's yours!"

The ghost laughs like a baby at the sight of a teat. "Try and take it off then."

The student tries. He tears at the crown, he flings his head upward, backward, sideways, pulls and pulls. His fingertips flame with the ferocious cold.

"How did *you* get rid of it?" he shrieks.

"I never put it on," replies the old writer.

"No, no, I mean the ghost, how did you get rid of the ghost!"

"I was going to tell you that, remember? But you ran off."

"You sent me away. It was a trick, you never meant to tell."

The ghost scolds: "No disputes!" And orders, "Tell now."

The student writhes; twists his neck; pulls and pulls. The crown stays on.

"The crown loosens," the old writer begins, "when the ghost goes. Everything dissolves together—"

"But *how?*"

"You find someone to give the crown to. That's all. You simply pass it on. All you do is agree to give away its powers to someone who wants it. Consider it a test of your own generosity."

"Who'll want it? Nobody wants such a thing!" the student shrieks. "It's stuck! Get it off! Off!"

"*You* wanted it."

"Prig! Moralist! *Ba'al ga'avah!* Didn't I come to you for advice? Literary advice, and instead you gave me this! I wanted help! You gave me metal junk! Sneak!"

"Interesting," observes the ghost, "that I myself acquired the crown in exactly the same way. I received it from Ibn

Gabirol. Via ouija board. I was skeptical about the method but discovered it to be legitimate. I consulted him about some of his verse-forms. To be specific, the problem of enjambment, which is more difficult in Hebrew than in some other languages. By way of reply he gave me the crown. Out of the blue it appeared on the board—naked, so to speak, and shining oddly, like a fish without scales. Of course there wasn't any ghost attached to the crown then. I'm the first, and you don't think I *like* having to materialize thirty minutes after someone's put it on? What I need is to be left in peace in Paradise, not this business of being on call the moment someone—"

"Ibn Gabirol?" the old writer breaks in, panting, all attention. Ibn Gabirol! Sublime poet, envied beyond envy, sublimeness without heir, who would not covet the crown of Ibn Gabirol?

"He said *he* got it from Isaiah. The quality of ownership keeps declining apparently. That's why they have me on patrol. If someone unworthy acquires it—well, that's where I put on my emanations and dig in. Come on," says the ghost, all at once sounding American, "let's go." He gives the student one of his snowflake shoves. "Where you go, I go. Where I go, you go. Now that you know the ropes, let's get out of here and find somebody who deserves it. Give it to some goy for a change. 'The righteous among the Gentiles are as judges in Israel.' My own suggestion is Oxford, Mississippi, Faulkner, William."

"Faulkner's dead."

"He is? I ought to look him up. All right then. Someone not so fancy. Norman Mailer."

"A Jew," sneers the student.

"Can you beat that. Never mind, we'll find someone. Keep away from the rot of Europe—Kafka had it once.

Maybe a black. An Indian. Spic maybe. We'll go to America and look."

Moistly the old writer plucks at the ghost. "Listen, this doesn't cancel the Prize? I still get it?"

"In two years you're in Stockholm."

"And me?" cries the student. "What about me? What happens to me?"

"You wear the crown until you get someone to take it from you. Blockhead! Dotard! Don't you *listen?*" says the ghost: his accent wobbles, he elides like a Calcuttan educated in Paris.

"No one wants it! I told you! Anyone who really needs it you'll say doesn't deserve it. If he's already famous he doesn't need it, and if he's unknown you'll think he degrades it. Like me. Not fair! There's no *way* to pass it on."

"You've got a point." The ghost considers this. "That makes sense. Logic."

"So get it off me!"

"However, again you forget lust. Lust overcomes logic."

"Stop! Off!"

"The King of Sweden," muses the old writer, "speaks no Hebrew. That will be a difficulty. I suppose I ought to begin to study Swedish."

"Off! Off!" yells the student. And tugs at his head, yanks at the crown, pulling, pulling, seizing it by the cold points. He throws himself down, wedges his legs against the writer's desk, tumbling after leverage; nothing works. Then methodically he kneels, lays his head on the floor, and methodically begins to beat the crown against the wooden floor. He jerks, tosses, taps, his white head in the brilliant crown is a wild flashing hammer; then he catches at his chest; his knuckles explode; then again he beats, beats, beats the crown down. But it stays stuck, no blow can knock it free. He beats. He heaves his head. Sparks spring from the crown, small lightnings leap. Oh, his chest, his ribs, his heart! The vial, where is the vial? His hands squirm toward his throat, his chest, his pocket. And his head beats the crown down against the floor. The old head halts, the head falls, the crown stays stuck, the heart is dead.

"Expired," says the ghost of Tchernikhovsky.

Well, that should be enough. No use making up any more of it. Why should I? It is not my story. It is not the goat's story. It is no one's story. It is a story nobody wrote, nobody wants, it has no existence. What does the notion of a *ba'al ga'avah* have to do with a silver crown? One belongs to morals, the other to magic. Stealing from two disparate tales I smashed their elements one into the other. Things must be brought together. In magic all divergences are linked and locked. The fact is I forced the crown onto the ambitious student in order to punish.

To punish? Yes. In life I am, though obscure, as generous and reasonable as those whom wide glory has sweetened; earlier you saw how generously and reasonably I dealt with the goat. So I am used to being taken for everyone's support, confidante, and consolation—it did not surprise me, propped there against that wall in the dark, when the goat begged me to read his story. Why should he not? My triumph is that, in my unrenown, everyone trusts me not to lie. But I always lie. Only on paper I do not lie. On paper I punish, I am malignant.

For instance: I killed off the student to punish him for arrogance. But it is really the goat I am punishing. It is an excellent thing to punish him. Did he not make his hero a student at the yeshiva, did he not make him call himself "religious"? But what is that? What is it to be "religious"? Is religion any different from magic? Whoever intends to separate them ends in proving them to be the same.

The goat was a *ba'al ga'avah!* I understood that only a *ba'al ga'avah* would dare to write about "religion."

So I punished him for it. How? By transmuting piety into magic.

Then—and I require you to accept this with the suddenness I myself experienced it: *as if by magic*—again I was drawn to look into the goat's story; and found, on the next-to-last page, an address. He had rubbed out (I have already mentioned this) his name; but here was a street and a number:

> **18 Herzl Street**
> **Brooklyn, N.Y.**

A street fashioned—so to speak—after the Messiah. Here I will halt you once more to ask you to take no notice of the implications of the goat's address. It is an aside worthy of the goat himself. It is he, not I, who would grab you by the sleeve here and now in order to explain exactly who Theodor Herzl was—oh, how I despise writers who will stop a story dead for the sake of showing off! Do you care whether or not Maimonides (supposing you had ever heard of that lofty saint) tells us that the messianic age will be recognizable simply by the resumption of Jewish political independence? Does it count if, by that definition, the Messiah turns out to be none other than a Viennese journalist of the last century? Doubtless Herzl was regarded by his contemporaries as a *ba'al ga'avah* for brazening out, in a modern moment, a Hebrew principality. And who is more of a *ba'al ga'avah* than the one who usurps the Messiah's own job?

Take Isaiah—was not Isaiah a *ba'al ga'avah* when he declared against observance—"I hate your feasts and your new moons"—and in the voice, no less, of the Creator Himself?

But thank God I have no taste for these notions. Already you have seen how earnestly my mind is turned toward hatred of metaphysical speculation. Practical action is my whole concern, and I have nothing but contempt for significant allusions, nuances, buried effects.

Therefore you will not be astonished at what I next undertook to do. I went—ha!—to the street of the Messiah to find the goat.

It was a place where there had been conflagrations. Rubble tentatively stood: brick on brick, about to fall. One remaining configuration of wall, complete with windows but no panes. The sidewalk underfoot stirred with crumbs, as of sugar grinding: mortar reduced to sand. A desert flushed over tumbled yards. Lintels and doors burned out, foundations squared like pebbles on a beach: in this spot once there had been cellars, stoops, houses. The smell of burned wood wandered. A civilization of mounds—who had lived here? Jews. There were no buildings left. A rectangular stucco fragment—of what? synagogue maybe—squatted in a space. There was no Number 18—only bad air, light flying in the gape and gash where the fires had driven down brick, mortar, wood, mothers, fathers, children pressing library cards inside their pockets—gone, finished.

And immediately—as if by magic—the goat!

"You!" I hooted, exactly as, in the story that never was, the old writer had cried it to Tchernikhovsky's shade.

"You've read my stuff," he said, gratified. "I knew you could find me easy if you wanted to. All you had to do was want to."

"Where do you live?"

"Number 18. I knew you'd want to."

"There isn't any 18."

He pointed. "It's what's left of the shul. No plumbing, but it still has a good kitchen in the back. I'm what you call a squatter, you don't mind?"

"Why should I mind?"

"Because I stole the idea from a book. It's this story about a writer who lives in an old tenement with his type-writer and the tenement's about to be torn down—"

The famous author who had written about the magic crown had written that story too; I reflected how some filch their fiction from life, others filch their lives from fiction. What people call inspiration is only pilferage. "You're not living in a tenement," I corrected, "you're living in a syna-gogue."

"What used to be. It's a hole now, a sort of cave. The Ark is left though, you want to see the Ark?"

I followed him through shards. There was no front door.

"What happened to this neighborhood?" I said.

"The Jews went away."

"Who came instead?"

"Fire."

The curtain of the Ark dangled in charred shreds. I peered inside the orifice which had once closeted the Scrolls: all blackness there, and the clear sacrificial smell of things that have been burned.

"See?" he said. "The stove works. It's the old wood-burn-ing kind. For years they didn't use it here, it just sat. And now—resurrection." Ah: the clear sacrificial smell was po-tatoes baking.

"Don't you have a job?"

"I write, I'm a writer. And no rent to pay anyhow."

"How do you drink?"

"You mean *what*." He held up a full bottle of Schapiro's kosher wine. "They left a whole case intact."

"But you can't wash, you can't even use the toilet."

"I pee and do my duty in the yard. Nobody cares. This is freedom, lady."

"Dirt," I said.

"What's dirt to Peter is freedom to Paul. Did you like my story? Sit."

There was actually a chair, but it had a typewriter on it. The goat did not remove it.

"How do you take a bath?" I persisted.

"Sometimes I go to my cousin's. I told you. The rabbi's wife."

"The rabbi from this synagogue?"

"No, he's moved to Woodhaven Boulevard. That's Queens. All the Jews from here went to Queens, did you know that?"

"*What* rabbi's wife?" I blew out, exasperated.

"I *told* you. The one with the crown. The one they wrote about in the papers. The one *he* lifted the idea of that story from. A rip-off that was, my cousin ought to sue."

Then I remembered. "All stories are rip-offs," I said. "Shakespeare stole his plots. Dostoyevski dug them out of the newspaper. Everybody steals. *The Decameron*'s stolen. Whatever looks like invention is theft."

"Great," he said, "that's what I need. Literary talk."

"What did you mean, you knew I would want to come? —Believe me, I didn't come for literary talk."

"You bet. You came because of my cousin. You came because of the crown."

I was amazed: instantly it coursed in on me that this was true. I had come because of the crown; I was in pursuit of the crown.

I said: "I don't care about the crown. I'm interested in the rabbi himself. The crown-blesser. What I care about is the psychology of the thing."

This word—"psychology"—made him cackle. "He's in jail, I thought you knew that. They got him for fraud."

"Does his wife still have any crowns around?"

"One."

"Here's your story," I said, handing it over. "Next time leave your name in. You don't have to obliterate it, rely on the world for that."

The pus on his eyelids glittered. "Alex will obliterate the world, not vice versa."

"How? By bombing it with stories? The first anonymous obliteration. The Flood without a by-line," I said. "At least everything God wrote was publishable. Alex what?"

"Goldflusser."

"You're a liar."

"Silbertsig."

"Cut it out."

"Kupferman. Bleifischer. Bettler. Kenigman."

"All that's mockery. If your name's a secret—"

"I'm lying low, hiding out, they're after me because I helped with the crowns."

I speculated, "You're the one who made them."

"No. She did that."

"Who?"

"My cousin. The rabbi's wife. She crocheted them. What he did was go buy the form—you get it from a costume loft, stainless steel. She used to make these little pointed sort of *gloves* for it, to protect it, see, and the shine would glimmer through, and then the customer would get to keep the crown-cover, as a sort of guarantee—"

"My God," I said, "what's all that about, why didn't *she* go to jail?"

"Crocheting isn't a crime."

"And you?" I said. "What did you do in all that?"

"Get customers. Fraudulent solicitation, that's a crime."

He took the typewriter off the chair and sat down. The wisp of beard wavered. "Didn't you like my story?" he accused. The pages were pressed with an urgency between his legs.

"No. It's all fake. It doesn't matter if you've been to Jerusalem. You've got the slant of the place all wrong. It doesn't matter about the yeshiva either. It doesn't matter if you really went to see some old geezer over there, you didn't get anything right. It's a terrible story."

"Where do you come off with that stuff?" he burst out. "Have *you* been to Jerusalem? Have *you* seen the inside of a yeshiva?"

"No."

"So!"

"I can tell when everything's fake," I said. "What I mean by fake is raw. When no one's ever used it before, it's something new under the sun, a whole new combination, that's bad. A real story is whatever you can predict, it has to be familiar, anyhow you have to know how it's going to come out, no exotic new material, no unexpected flights—"

He rushed out at me: "What you want is to bore people!"

"I'm a very boring writer," I admitted; out of politeness I kept from him how much his story, and even my own paraphrase of it, had already bored me. "But in *principle* I'm right. The only good part in the whole thing was explaining about the *ba'al ga'avah*. People hate to read foreign words, but at least it's ancient wisdom. Old, old stuff."

Then I told him how I had redesigned his story to include a ghost.

He opened the door of the stove and threw his manuscript in among the black-skinned potatoes.

"Why did you do that?"

"To show you I'm no *ba'al ga'avah*. I'm humble enough to burn up what somebody doesn't like."

I said suspiciously, "You've got other copies."

"Sure. Other potatoes too."

"Look," I said, riding malice, "it took me two hours to find this place, I have to go to the yard."

"You want to take a leak? Come over to my cousin's. It's not far. My cousin's lived in this neighborhood sixty years."

Furiously I went after him. He was a crook leading me to the house of crooks. We walked through barrenness and canker, a ruined city, store-windows painted black, one or two curtained by gypsies, some boarded, barred, barbed, old newspapers rolling in the gutter, the sidewalks speckled with viscous blotch. Overhead a smell like kerosene, the breath of tenements. The cousin's toilet stank as if no one had flushed it in half a century; it had one of those tanks high up, attached to the ceiling, a perpetual drip running down the pull chain. The sink was in the kitchen. There was no soap; I washed my hands with Ajax powder while the goat explained me to his cousin.

"She's interested in the crown," he said.

"Out of business," said the cousin.

"Maybe for her."

"Not doing business, that's all. For nobody whatsoever."

"I'm not interested in buying one," I said, "just in finding out."

"Crowns is against the law."

"For healing," the goat argued, "not for showing. She knows the man who wrote that story. You remember about that guy, I told you, this famous writer who took—"

"Who took! Too much fame," said the cousin, "is why Saul sits in jail. Before newspapers and stories we were left

in peace, we helped people peacefully." She condemned me
with an oil-surfaced eye, the colorless slick of the ripening
cataract. "My husband, a holy man, him they put in jail.
Him! A whole year, twelve months! A man like that! Brains,
a saint—"

"But he fooled people," I said.

"In helping is no fooling. Out, lady. You had to pee, you
peed. You needed a public facility, very good, now out. I
don't look for extra customers for my toilet bowl."

"Goodbye," I said to the goat.

"You think there's hope for me?"

"Quit writing about ideas. Stay out of the yeshiva, watch
out for religion. Don't make up stories about famous writers."

"Listen," he said—his nose was speckled with pustules of
lust, his nostrils gaped—"you didn't like that one, I'll give
you another. I've got plenty more, I've got a crateful."

"What are you talking," said the cousin.

"She knows writers," he said, "in person. She knows how
to get things published."

I protested, "I can hardly get published myself—"

"You published something?" said the cousin.

"A few things, not much."

"Alex, bring Saul's box."

"That's not the kind of stuff," the goat said.

"Definitely. About expression I'm not so concerned like
you. What isn't so regular, anyone with a desire and a pencil
can fix it."

The goat remonstrated, "What Saul has is something
else, it's not *writing*—"

"With connections," said the cousin, "nothing is something else, everything is writing. Lady, in one box I got my
husband's entire holy life work. The entire theory of healing
and making the dead ones come back for a personal appear-

ance. We sent maybe to twenty printing houses, nothing
doing. You got connections, I'll show you something."

"Print," I reminded her, "is what you said got the rabbi in
trouble."

"Newspapers. Lies. False fame. Everything with a twist.
You call him rabbi, who made from him a rabbi? The entire
world says rabbi, so let it be rabbi. There he sits in jail, a
holy man what did nothing his whole life to harm. Whatever
a person asked for, this was what he gave. Whatever you
wanted to call him, this was what he became. Alex! Take out
Saul's box, it's in the bottom of the dresser with the crown."

"The crown?" I said.

"The crown is nothing. What's something is Saul's brain.
Alex!"

The goat shut his nostrils. He gave a snicker and disap-
peared. Through the kitchen doorway I glimpsed a sagging
bed and heard a drawer grind open.

He came back lugging a carton with a picture of tomato
cans on it. On top of it lay the crown. It was gloved in a
green pattern of peephole diamonds.

"Here," said the cousin, "is Saul's ideas. Listen, that
famous writer what went to steal from the papers—a fool. If
he could steal what's in Saul's brain, what would he need a
newspaper? Read!" She dipped a fist into a hiss of sheets and
foamed up a sheaf of them. "You'll see, the world will rush to
put in print. The judge at the trial—I said to him, look in
Saul's box, you'll see the truth, no fraud. If they would read
Saul's papers, not only would he not sit in jail, the judge
with hair growing from his ears they would throw out!"

I looked at the goat; he was not laughing. He reached
out and put the crown on my head.

It felt lighter than I imagined. It was easy to forget you
were wearing it.

I read:

Why does menkind not get what they wish for? This is an easy solution. He is used to No. Always No. So it comes he is afraid to ask.

"The power of positive thinking," I said. "A philosopher."

"No, no," the cousin intervened, "not a philosopher, what do philosophers know to heal, to make real shadows from the dead?"

Through thinning threads of beard the goat said, "Not a philosopher."

I read:

Everything depends what you ask. Even you're not afraid to ask, plain asking is not sufficient. If you ask in a voice, there got to be an ear to listen in. The ear of Ha-shem, King of the Universe. (His Name we don't use it every minute like a shoelace.) A Jew don't go asking Ha-shem for inside information, for what reason He did this, what ideas He got on that, how come He let happen such-and-such a pogrom, why a good person loved by one and all dies with cancer, and a lousy bastard he's rotten to his partner and cheats and plays the numbers, this fellow lives to 120. With questions like this don't expect no replies, Ha-shem don't waste breath on trash from fleas. Ha-shem says, My secrets are My secrets, I command you what you got to do, the rest you leave to Me. This is no news that He don't reveal His deepest business. From that territory you get what you deserve, silence.

"What are you up to?" said the goat.

"Silence."

"Ssh!" said the cousin. "Alex, so let her read in peace!"

For us, not one word. He shuts up, His mouth is locked. So how come G-d conversed in history with Adam, with Abraham, with Moses? All right, you can argue that Moses and Abraham was worth it to G-d to listen to, what they said Ha-shem wanted to hear. After all they fed Him back His own ideas. An examination, and already they knew the answers. Smart guys, in the whole history of menkind no one else like these couple of guys. But with Adam, new and naked with no clothes on, just when the whole world was born, was Adam different from me and you? What did Adam know? Even right from wrong he didn't know yet. And still G-d thought, to Adam it's worthwhile to say a few words, I'm not wasting my breath. So what was so particular about Adam that he got Ha-shem's attention, and as regards me and you He don't blink an eye? Adam is better than me and you? We don't go around like a nudist colony, between good and lousy we already know what's what, with or without apples. To me and you G-d should also talk!

"You're following?" the cousin urged. "You see what's in Saul's brain? A whole box full like this, and sits in jail!"

But when it comes wishes, when it comes dreams, who says No? Who says Ha-shem stops talking? Wishes, dreams, imaginations —like fishes in the head. Ha-shem put in Joseph's head two good dreams, were they lies? The truth and nothing but the truth! Q.E.D. To Adam Ha-shem spoke one way, and when He finishes with Moses he talks another way. In a dream, in a wish. That *epikoros* Sigmund Freud, he also figured this out. Whomever says Sigmund Freud stinks from sex, they're mistaken. A wish is the voice, a dream is the voice, an imagination is the voice, all is the voice of Ha-shem the Creator. Naturally a voice is a biological thing, who says No? Whatsoever happens inside the human is a biological thing.

"What are you up to?" the goat asked again.
"Biology."
"Don't laugh: A man walked in here shaking all over, he walked out okay, I saw it myself."
The cousin said mournfully, "A healer."

"I wrote a terrific story about that guy, I figured what he had was cystic fibrosis, I can show you—"

"There isn't any market for medical stories," I said.

"This was a miracle story."

"There are no miracles."

"That's right!" said the cousin. She dug down again into the box. "One time only, instead of plain writing down, Saul made up a story on this subject exactly. On a yellow piece paper. Aha, here. Alex, read aloud."

The goat read:

One night in the middle of dim stars Ha-shem said, No more miracles! An end with miracles, I already did enough, from now on nothing.

So a king makes an altar and bows down. "O Ha-shem, King of the Universe, I got a bad war on my hands and I'm taking a beating. Make a miracle and save the whole country." Nothing doing, no miracle.

Good, says Ha-shem, this is how it's going to be from now on.

So along comes the Germans, in the camp they got a father and a little son maybe twelve years old. And the son is on the list to be gassed tomorrow. So the father runs around to find a German to bribe, G-d knows what he's got to bribe him with, maybe his wife's diamond ring that he hid somewhere and they didn't take it away yet. And he fixes up the whole thing, tomorrow he'll bring the diamond to the German and they'll take the boy off the list and they won't kill him. They'll slip in some other boy instead and who will know the difference?

Well, so that could be the end, but it isn't. All day after everything's fixed up, the father is thinking and thinking, and in the middle of the night he goes to an old rabbi that's in the camp also, and he tells the rabbi he's going to save his little son.

And the rabbi says, "So why come to me? You made your decision already." The father says, "Yes, but they'll put another boy in his place." The rabbi says, "Instead of Isaac, Abraham put a ram. And that was for G-d. You put another child, and for what? To feed Moloch." The father asks, "What is the law on this?" "The law is, Don't kill."

The next day the father don't bring the bribe. And his eyes don't never see his beloved little child again. Well, so that could be the end, but it isn't. Ha-shem looks at what's happening, here is a man what didn't save his own boy so he wouldn't be responsible with killing someone else. Ha-shem says to Himself, I made a miracle anyhow. I blew in one man so much power of My commandments that his own flesh and blood he lets go to Moloch, so long he shouldn't kill. That I created even one such person like this is a very great miracle, and I didn't even notice I was doing it. So now positively no more.

And after this the destruction continues, no interruptions. Not only the son is gassed, but also the father, and also the boy what they would have put in his place. And also and also and also, until millions of bones of alsos goes up in smoke. About miracles Ha-shem don't change his mind except by accident. So the question menkind has to ask their conscience is this: If the father wasn't such a good commandment-keeper that it's actually a miracle to find a man like this left in the world, what could happen instead? And if only one single miracle could slip through before G-d notices it, which one? Suppose this father didn't use up the one miracle, suppose the miracle is that G-d will stop the murderers altogether, suppose! Instead: nothing doing, the father on account of one kid eats up the one miracle that's lying around loose. For the sake of one life, the whole world is lost.

But on this subject, what's written in our holy books? What the sages got to say? The sages say different: If you save one life only, it's like the whole world is saved. So which is true? Naturally, whatever's written is what's true. What does this prove?

It proves that if you talk miracle, that's when everything becomes false. Men and women! Remember! No stories from miracles! No stories and no belief!

"You see?" said the cousin. "Here you have Saul's theories exactly. Whoever says miracles, whoever says magic, tells a lie. On account of a lie a holy man sits in a cage."

"And the crown?" I asked.

She ignored this. "You'll help to publish. You'll give to the right people, you'll give to connections—"

"But why? Why do you need this?"

"What's valuable you give away, you don't keep it for yourself. Listen, is the Bible a secret? The whole world takes from it. Is Talmud a secret? Whatever's a lie should be a secret, not what's holy and true!"

I appealed to the goat. He was licking his fingertips. "I can't digest any of this—"

"You haven't had a look at Saul," he said, "that's why."

The cousin said meanly, "I saw you put on her the crown."

"She wants it."

"The crown is nothing."

"She wants it."

"Then show her Saul."

"You mean in prison?" I said.

"In the bedroom on the night table."

The goat fled. This time he returned carrying a small gilded tin frame. In it was a snapshot of another bearded man.

"Look closely."

But instead of examining the photograph, I all at once wanted to study the goat's cousin. She was one of those tiny twig-thin old women who seem to enlarge the more you get used to their voices. It was as if her whine and her whirr were a pump, and pumped her up; she was now easily as tall as I (though I am myself not very tall) and expanding curiously. She was wearing a checked nylon housedress and white socks in slippers, above which bulged purplish varicose nodules. Her eyes were terribly magnified by metal-rimmed lenses, and looked out at me with the vengefulness of a pair of greased platters. I was astonished to see that a chromium crown had buried itself among the strings of her wandering hairs: having been too often dyed ebony, they were slipping out of their follicles and onto her collarbone. She had an exaggerated widow's peak and was elsewhere a little bit bald.

The goat too wore a crown.

"I thought there was only one left," I objected.

"Look at Saul, you'll see the only one."

The man in the picture wore a silver crown. I recognized him, though the light was shut off in him and the space of his flesh was clearly filled.

"Who is this?" I said.

"Saul."

"But I've seen him!"

"That's right," the cousin said.

"Because you wanted to," said the goat.

"The ghost I put in your story," I reminded him, "this is what it looked like."

The cousin breathed. "You published that story?"

"It's not even written down."

"Whose ghost was it?" asked the goat.

"Tchernikhovsky's. The Hebrew poet. A *ba'al ga'avah*. He wrote a poem called 'Before the Statue of Apollo.' In the last line God is bound with leather thongs."

"Who binds him?"

"The Jews. With their phylacteries. I want to read more," I said.

The two of them gave me the box. The little picture they set on the kitchen table, and they stood over me in their twinkling crowns while I splashed my hands through the false rabbi's stories. Some were already browning at the margins, in ink turned violet, some were on lined school paper, written with a ball-point pen. About a third were in Yiddish; there was even a thin notebook all in Russian; but most were pressed out in pencil in an immigrant's English on all kinds of odd loose sheets, the insides of old New Year greeting cards, the backs of cashiers' tapes from the supermarket, in one instance the ripped-out leather womb of an old wallet.

Saul's ideas were:

sorcery, which he denied.
levitation, which he doubted.
magic, which he sneered at.
miracles, which he denounced.
healing, which he said belonged in hospitals.
instant cures, which he said were fancies and delusions.
the return of deceased loved ones, which he said were wishful
    hallucinations.
the return of dead enemies, which ditto.
plural gods, which he disputed.
demons, which he derided.
amulets, which he disparaged and repudiated.
Satan, from which hypothesis he scathingly dissented.

He ridiculed everything. He was a rationalist.

"It's amazing," I said, "that he looks just like Tchernikhovsky."

"What does Tchernikhovsky look like?" one of the two crowned ones asked me; I was no longer sure which.

"I don't know, how should I know? Once I saw his picture in an anthology of translations, but I don't remember it.
Why are there so many crowns in this room? What's the
point of these crowns?"

Then I found the paper on crowns:

You take a real piece mineral, what kings wear. You put it on,
you become like a king. What you wish, you get. But what you
get you shouldn't believe in unless it's real. How do you know
when something's real? If it lasts. How long? This depends. If
you wish for a Pyramid, it should last as long like a regular
Pyramid lasts. If you wish for long life, it should last as long
like your own grandfather. If you wish for a Magic Crown, it
should last as long like the brain what it rests on.

I interrupted myself: "Why doesn't he wish himself out
of prison? Why didn't he wish himself out of getting sen-
tenced?"

"He lets things take their course."

Then I found the paper on things taking their course:

From my own knowledge I knew a fellow what loved a woman,
Beylinke, and she died. So he looked and looked for a twin to
this Beylinke, and it's no use, such a woman don't exist. Instead
he married a different type altogether, and he made her change
her name to Beylinke and make love on the left side, like the
real Beylinke. And if he called Beylinke! and she forgot to answer
(her name was Ethel) he gave her a good knock on the back,
and one day he knocked hard into the kidney and she got a
growth and she died. And all he got from his forcing was a lone-
some life.

Everything is according to destiny, you can't change nothing. Not
that anybody can know what happens before it happens, not even
Ha-shem knows which dog will bite which cat next week in
Persia.

"Enough," said one of the two in the crowns. "You read and you took enough. You ate enough and you drank enough from this juice. Now you got to pay."

"To pay?"

"The payment is, to say thank you what we showed you everything, you take and you publish."

"Publishing isn't the same as Paradise."

"For some of us it is," said one.

"She knows from Paradise!" scoffed the other.

They thrust the false rabbi's face into my face.

"It isn't English, it isn't even coherent, it's inconsistent, it's crazy, nothing hangs together, nobody in his right mind would—"

"Connections you got."

"No."

"That famous writer."

"A stranger."

"Then somebody else."

"There's no one. I can't make magic—"

"*Ba'al ga'avah!* You're better than Saul? Smarter? Cleverer? You got better ideas? You, a nothing, they print, and he sits in a box?"

"I looked up one of your stories. It stank, lady. The one called 'Usurpation.' Half of it's swiped, you ought to get sued. You don't know when to stop. You swipe other people's stories and you go on and on, on and on, I fell asleep over it. Boring! Long-winded!"

The mass of sheets pitched into my lap. My fingers flashed upward: there was the crown, with its crocheted cover, its blunted points. Little threads had gotten tangled in my hair. If I tugged, the roots would shriek. Tchernikhovsky's paper eyes looked frightened. Crevices opened on either side of his nose and from the left nostril the gray bone of his skull poked out, a cheekbone like a pointer.

"I don't have better ideas," I said. "I'm not interested in ideas, I don't care about ideas. I hate ideas. I only care about stories."

"Then take Saul's stories!"

"Trash. Justice and mercy. He tells you how to live, what to do, the way to think. Righteousness fables, morality tales. Didactic stuff. Rabbinical trash," I said. "What I mean is *stories*. Even you," I said to the goat, "wanting to write about writers! Morality, mortality! You people eat yourself up with morality and mortality!"

"What else should a person eat?"

Just then I began to feel the weight of the crown. It pressed unerringly into the secret tunnels of my brain. A pain like a grief leaped up behind my eyes, up through the temples, up, up, into the marrow of the crown. Every point of it was a spear, a nail. The crown was no different from the bone of my head. The false rabbi Tchernikhovsky tore himself from the tin prison of his frame and sped to the ceiling as if gassed. He had bluish teeth and goblin's wings made of brown leather. Except for the collar and cravat that showed in the photograph, below his beard he was naked. His testicles were leathery. His eyeballs were glass, like a doll's. He was solid as a doll; I was not so light-headed as to mistake him for an apparition. His voice was as spindly as a harpsichord: "Choose!"

"Between what and what?"

"The Creator or the creature. God or god. The Name of Names or Apollo."

"Apollo," I said on the instant.

"Good," he tinkled, "blessings," he praised me, "flowings and flowings, streams, brooks, lakes, waters out of waters."

Stories came from me then, births and births of tellings, narratives and suspenses, turning-points and palaces, foam of the sea, mermen sewing, dragons pullulating out of quicksilver, my mouth was a box, my ears flowed, they gushed legends and tales, none of them of my own making, all of them acquired, borrowed, given, taken, inherited, stolen, plagiarized, usurped, chronicles and sagas invented at the beginning of the world by the offspring of giants copulating with the daughters of men. A king broke out of the shell of my left eye and a queen from the right one, the box of my belly lifted its scarred lid to let out frogs and swans, my womb was cleft and stories burst free of their balls of blood. Stories choked the kitchen, crept up the toilet tank, replenished the bedroom, knocked off the goat's crown, knocked off the cousin's crown, my own crown in its coat contended with the vines and tangles of my hair, the false rabbi's beard had turned into strips of leather, into whips, the whips struck at my crown, it slid to my forehead, the whips curled round my arm, the crown sliced the flesh of my forehead.

At last it fell off.

The cousin cried out her husband's name.

"Alex," I called to the goat: the name of a conqueror, Aristotle's pupil, the arrogant god-man.

In the hollow streets which the Jews had left behind there were scorched absences, apparitions, usurpers. Someone had broken the glass of the kosher butcher's abandoned window and thrown in a pig's head, with anatomical tubes still dripping from the neck.

When we enter Paradise there will be a cage for story-writers, who will be taught as follows:

All that is not Law is levity.

But we have not yet ascended. The famous writer has not. The goat has not. The false rabbi has not; he sits out his year. A vanity press is going to bring out his papers. The bill for editing, printing, and binding will be $1,847.45. The goat's cousin will pay for it from a purse in the bottom bowel of the night table.

The goat inhabits the deserted synagogue, drinking wine, littering the yard with his turds. Occasionally he attends a public reading. Many lusts live in his chin-hairs, like lice.

Only Tchernikhovsky and the shy old writer of Jerusalem have ascended. The old writer of Jerusalem is a fiction; murmuring psalms, he snacks on leviathan and polishes his Prize with the cuff of his sleeve. Tchernikhovsky eats nude at the table of the nude gods, clean-shaven now, his limbs radiant, his youth restored, his sex splendidly erect, the discs of his white ears sparkling, a convivial fellow; he eats without self-restraint from the celestial menu, and when the Sabbath comes (the Sabbath of Sabbaths, which flowers every seven centuries in the perpetual Sabbath of Eden), as usual he avoids the congregation of the faithful before the Footstool and the Throne. Then the taciturn little Canaanite idols call him, in the language of the spheres, kike.

(1973)

Obelisk